HOUND
DOG
TRUE

HOUND DOG TRUE

LINDA URBAN

HARCOURT CHILDREN'S BOOKS
Houghton Mifflin Harcourt
Boston   New York   2011

Harcourt Children's Books is an imprint of
Houghton Mifflin Harcourt Publishing Company.

www.hmhbooks.com

Text set in ITC Legacy Serif

Library of Congress Cataloging-in-Publication Data
Urban, Linda.
Hound dog true / Linda Urban.
p. cm.
Summary: Mattie, a shy fifth-grader, wants to hide out at her new school
by acting as apprentice to her Uncle Potluck, the custodian, but her plan
falls apart when she summons the courage to speak about what matters
most and finds a true friend.
ISBN 978-0-547-99609-7
[1. Bashfulness—Fiction. 2. Friendship—Fiction. 3. Janitors—Fiction. 4.
Family life—Fiction. 5. Schools—Fiction. 6. Moving, Household—Fiction.]
I. Title.
PZ7.U637Hou 2011
[Fic]—dc22
2011009599

Manufactured in the United States of America
16 1083 18 17 16 15
4500535276   ^ B C D E F G

For Julio

Uncle Potluck said when he talked to the moon, the moon talked back.

Mama laughed. "Same old Potluck," she said, but he'd already grabbed his hat. Already looked at Mattie, eyebrows up, saying, "It's hound dog true." Already opened the door to the night.

Out they went, out past the bean tepees and tomato cages and the stone rabbit standing guard, Mattie matching Uncle Potluck's steps in the garden dirt. Out they went beyond the tangle of pumpkin vines and the backyard house Miss Sweet was renting.

"Few more days, you'll know this place by heart," Uncle Potluck said. "Won't need me showing you the way."

Mattie was not so sure. It was dark out here, without streetlights and golden arches and headlights graying up the sky. Uncle Potluck had grown up in this yard. Mama, too. Likely it would take till Mattie grew up before she could path her way through the night.

Up they went, up the rise to the edge of the woods,

to the flat rock ledge by the apple tree. Uncle Potluck looked up and Mattie looked up, up to where the moon ought to be. Uncle Potluck whispered, "She's hiding behind the skirts of Mama Night, you know?"

Mattie knew.

Uncle Potluck leaped up on that rock. Put his hat to his heart. "Miss Moon," he called. "Miss Moon, come on out, sweetheart."

Uncle Potluck waited and Mattie waited till a breeze came by, thinning the clouds.

"You've got to trust the moon, if you want the moon to trust you," he said, handing Mattie his hat.

He wanted her to talk, Mattie knew. Wanted her to introduce herself, say something fine, but Mattie could not find a word in that dark.

She put on Uncle Potluck's hat, let it fall down over her eyes.

What did Mattie have to say that would interest the moon?

CHAPTER ONE

THE STICK MAN HAS BOLTS of cartoon electricity shooting out of him. *Attention! Avertissement!* it says over his head. *Atención! Achtung! Do not use ladder in electrical storms. May cause severe injury or death.*

Mattie is glad she is not in an electrical storm. She does not want little bolts of lightning to shoot out of her. Of course, she's just standing at the bottom of the ladder, holding it two-hand steady, eyes level with the warning labels pasted to its metal sides. It's Uncle Potluck up top, like the stick man, so probably Uncle Potluck would get the death. Mattie'd only get severe injury, she figures, and for a minute she thinks about what kind of injury that might be. Lightning could split a tree, she knew. Maybe it would split her. Take a leg off or something. Or maybe she'd singe all over, like a shirt ironed too hot. Either way, it is good they are inside, she tells herself.

It is good that they are here, inside Mitchell P. Anderson Elementary School, inside Ms. Morgan's fifth grade classroom, inside the room that Uncle Potluck says will be hers once school starts.

It is good, she tells herself again.

And she keeps it good by focusing on the stick man, not wandering her eyes to the rows of desks or the coat closet doors or the blackboard up front. She reminds herself there is a whole week before this new school starts and she doesn't have to think about any of that yet.

She can just help Uncle Potluck fulfill his Janitorial Oath.

She can steady the ladder.

She can think about severe injury and death.

"Mattie Mae," says Uncle Potluck. "I am entrusting you with this distinguished veteran." Mattie loosens one hand from the ladder and reaches for the light bulb Uncle Potluck hands down. It is not a regular bulb—not the round kind that might *ping* on above a stick man if he got an idea. It is the long, skinny, lightsaber kind. The kind that sat in the ceilings of every school Mattie ever went to. Which is three. Four, counting this one. Four schools.

The bulb is ash gray. Uncle Potluck puts his hat to his heart and bows his head. "Gave its life in service of the illumination of youth," he says.

Mattie smiles. Bows her head like Uncle Potluck. "Thank you, bulb," she says. It's only Uncle Potluck around, so she doesn't mind saying it out loud.

"Put that in the box, Mattie. We'll take it back to Authorized Personnel and give it a proper burial." Mattie nods and lets go of the ladder. It doesn't wobble. Uncle Potluck doesn't need steadying, really. He's been performing the Custodial Arts since before Mattie was even born.

Up at the front of the room, a skinny box rests against Ms. Morgan's desk. Mattie sets the veteran down and slow-careful pulls a fresh bulb from that box, a bulb so white it matches the chalk on the blackboard ledge.

This is probably where she'll have to stand.

It's always up front that teachers make you stand.

Every time Mattie has been new at a school, the teacher made her stand in front of the blackboard and say her name. Except last time, fourth grade. That was Mrs. D'Angelo's class. Mrs. D'Angelo had a whiteboard instead. Told Mattie to stand in front of that while she wrote Mattie's name fat and loopy in blue marker on that whiteboard.

Introduce yourself.

"I'm Mattie Breen," Mattie had said.

Louder.

"I'm Mattie Breen." Came out quieter, though.

Tell us something about yourself.

And just like every other transfer day, Mattie got tangled in her own head, trying to figure out what would be good to say. What she could say that would be smart or funny or interesting enough to make people forget they already had friends and places to sit at lunch and people to be with at recess.

Mattie'd had her notebook with her—the first one, the yellow one—and she'd held it to her chest like armor. Tucked her chin behind it. Felt her breath bouncing hot back.

Shoes shuffled under chairs.

Shy, someone whispered.

Stuck up got whispered back.

Just the day before, Mattie had seen a TV show about Buddhist monks, how they could breathe so deep and slow they seemed to stop time, to stop their own hearts from beating. Mattie tried that then.

Breathed slow and deep, trying to stop her face from redding up.

It did not work.

Probably because I'm not a Buddhist, she thought. And that's what she said.

"I'm not a Buddhist."

That was enough for Mrs. D'Angelo to tell her she could *sit down.*

Mattie did sit down.

Sat holding her yellow notebook at a table Mrs. D'Angelo had pushed an extra chair up to.

Sat in the place Mrs. D'Angelo said was *for now.*

Sat with four other kids—one of them that girl Star, though Mattie didn't know that yet. All Mattie knew was that she had said, *Not a Buddhist.*

Not exactly the kind of introduction that would have people rushing to make friends.

Not that she knew how to make friends, really.

She could be friend*ly*, of course. After the newness of a place wore off, she'd been friend*ly*. By then it was usually too late for true, tell-your-secrets-to friends, even the nicest people calling her *that shy girl* instead of Mattie.

Not a Buddhist.

Not a Buddhist. Not a Buddhist. Not a Buddhist.

Took a whole half of that morning before she could concentrate on anything else.

When finally she did settle, Mattie caught a glimpse of the whiteboard. There was her name sitting bold and friendly among the times tables and the spelling words. Like she was a lesson. Like Mattie Breen being bold-friendly was just as true as five times five being twenty-five or *weird* being spelled the way it was.

I'm Mattie Breen, she thought.

She sat straighter.

I'm bold and friendly, she thought. *Fact-true, like it says on the board.*

That's when Mrs. D'Angelo started in on science. Started writing *Survival* on the board. Writing *of the*. Finding no room left on that big whiteboard for *fittest*.

"Forgive me, Mattie," she said, smiling.

And then Mattie Breen got erased.

CHAPTER TWO

UNCLE POTLUCK SLIDES the new bulb into its socket and slips the gray cover into its place among the ceiling tiles. Mattie has to move so he can step down the ladder, but she's close enough to hear the hooting sound he makes on the third step.

It's his traitorous knee that makes him hoot, the tiny sting of it when he's taking stairs or kneeling or getting up from having sat still for a movie. He's got surgery planned for a few months from now, come Christmas vacation. That's why this move was back to Uncle Potluck's, to the house where he and Mama and their brothers grew up.

"I've planned it all out," Mama told Mattie. "Potluck will need some help around Christmas. By then I'll have some vacation time, and you'll be all settled in and comfortable at school." Mama's first two fingers fluttered on her thumb, like the piccolo player Mattie had seen once. Except when the piccolo man did it, he was making music. When Mama's fingers moved that way it meant she was making plans, her fingers moving as fast as the thoughts in her head. "It was time for a new job, anyway. My old boss was getting grouchy and there was talk of layoffs. And when the going gets tough . . ."

Mama had waited then, like she always did. Waited for Mattie to say, ". . . the tough get going," which Mattie always said and Mama always took to mean that Mattie was fine with moving again, whether she was or not. This time, though, Mattie had been happy, since moving meant being with Uncle Potluck.

"Mattie?" Uncle Potluck clatters the ladder flat. Puts it to his shoulder. "Will you carry the decedent?"— by which he means for her to get the box with the old light bulb in it.

Down the main hallway of Mitchell P. Anderson Elementary they go. Uncle Potluck first, Mattie following. You can't tell he's got a traitorous knee when he's walking. He just walks, steady and strong, past the drinking fountain and the restrooms and the gymnasium/stage/cafeteria. At the administrative office, he stops long enough to salute the gold-framed picture of Principal Bonnet that hangs outside the door, and then they are off again, rounding the corner and heading to the end of the hall, past the art room, past the music room, to a pair of orange doors marked AUTHORIZED PERSONNEL. That's where Uncle Potluck keeps his office.

It is a neat office, with a desk tucked snug under the hot-water pipe and walls covered in pegboard. Uncle Potluck hangs his tools on those walls. He's drawn white lines around them, too—like the ones they draw around dead bodies on TV shows, except dead-body lines are about mysteries and Uncle Potluck's lines are about things being for sure where they belong. Broom in the broom spot. Wrench in the wrench spot. There's even an outline for Uncle Potluck's hat— though mostly that spot stays empty.

Things that don't belong on the walls have shelf spots or drawer spots, all of them labeled neat.

SCREWS
GLUE
TAPE

EXTENSION CORDS
STRING

Uncle Potluck's chair has a label, too. DIRECTOR OF CUSTODIAL ARTS it says on the back. Neat and square.

Mama is neat, too, Mattie thinks. But Mama's neat is about getting rid of things. Every time she and Mattie moved, things got left behind. Toasters and TV trays and Mattie's old dollhouse, all left by the driveway, a FREE sign propped against them. Mama never owns more than can fit in a pickup truck.

When Mattie was real little, she would buckle herself into the truck before any boxes got packed, afraid maybe there wouldn't be room for her. Used to think that was what had happened to her father, that he hadn't fit in the truck and Mama had driven off. Really, he was just too young to get married, so he drove off himself.

Mattie pushes the DIRECTOR OF CUSTODIAL ARTS chair up to the desk, so Uncle Potluck can maneuver the ladder. Watches him hang it firm in the ladder spot. Sees a spot marked RECYCLING and sets the bulb box there, which is exactly where it goes.

"Mattie Mae," Uncle Potluck says. "I have a mind

to declare you too talented for this here school and take you on as an apprentice." And it feels like Uncle Potluck has drawn a fat white belonging-line around her.

MATTIE MAE BREEN

CUSTODIAL APPRENTICE

CHAPTER THREE

THAT AFTERNOON MATTIE TAKES something shiny-silver out of her bureau, carries it to Uncle Potluck's rock ledge out on the rise. It is shady there now, but most of the day the rock has kept company with the sunshine, and the day-heat has soaked up into it. Mattie lies down flat on the rock, feeling the warmth of it on her belly. She places the silver thing in front of her.

It is a notebook.

A silver notebook with creamy white paper stitched into it—the kind a person would have to work real hard to tear a page out of.

It was a gift from Mama, given two weeks ago, on the very day she said they'd be moving again. "I thought you might want to write your feelings in it," Mama had said, but right off, Mattie knew that book was too fine for feelings. And she didn't write stories anymore. Not since Star.

Mattie didn't tell Mama that, though. Just said *thank you*.

Now, turns out, she does have something worth writing in that silver book.

Mattie Breen, Custodial Apprentice, she writes.

Her stomach flutters, same as Mama's fingers. This is how it feels to make a plan.

There are laws, Mattie knows.

There are laws that say she has to be in the classroom and learn fractions and spelling and survival of the fittest. But there are not laws about going outside at recess time. And there are not laws about where to sit at lunchtime.

And there are not laws that say you have to show up at the same exact time everybody else does and jostle around in the coatroom. You could go earlier. Your coat doesn't have to be with everybody else's coat.

It could have its own peg someplace else.

And your boots could rest someplace else, too.

If you were helpful to somebody—really, truly helpful, apprentice-like helpful—you could probably go help that person during all those lawless times.

Mattie turns the page, runs her finger down the center stitches. Her stomach flutters again.

Custodial Wisdom, she writes.

Underneath, she writes all the things she's learned—about custodial safety and being prepared, mostly. Like how as soon as you are done vacuuming, you are supposed to pull the plug from the socket and wind the cord snug up so nobody trips on it. And how before you do any mopping, you have to set out that yellow CAUTION pyramid.

There's a stick man on the pyramid, like the one on Uncle Potluck's ladder, except this stick man has one leg up in the air and his arms flung around with little motion parentheses. Like he's lost his footing, Mattie thinks, except he doesn't really have feet, just rounded spots at the ends of his legs. Makes sense he'd slide.

She doesn't write the footless part in her notebook. Just the serious part about putting out CAUTION pyramids and mopping and how when you're all done, you have to look back and make sure you didn't miss a spot or leave puddles orphaned anyplace. Either was an indication of faulty professionalism, Uncle Potluck said.

Mattie writes that down, too.

Faulty professionalism.

She will not be a faulty professional. She will spend the next four days writing and learning and being professional next to Uncle Potluck, proving herself worthy of being a true custodial apprentice. Proving how once school starts, he should keep her by his side, instead of making her go to lunch or recess or be with whatever wild kids might be at Mitchell P. Anderson Elementary.

That is Mattie's plan.

Four days of proving. And then on Saturday, or maybe Sunday, she'll talk to Uncle Potluck about it—apprentice to custodian. And on Monday she'll be able to introduce herself to her new class just fine.

I'm Mattie Breen.

I'm a custodial apprentice.

She can hear herself saying this bold and friendly, standing in front of the blackboard. Sees and hears it so much, she does not see or hear anything else.

Does not hear someone else coming up the rise toward her. Is not ready when the voice stabs out.

"What are you writing?"

Mattie feels herself spring from the rock, spill to

the grass, scramble upright. Out the side of her eye she sees a flash: her silver notebook turning in the air, pages exposed, falling to the ground.

A hand reaches for it, but Mattie grabs faster. *Mine*, she shouts, but only in her head.

Thumpthumpthump, the thump of her heartbeat matching the thud of her feet on the ground, already running down the rise, her head saying *stop* and *stupid* and *baby*, but she does not stop because her head is also already saying *too late now* and *too late now* and *too late now*, until she is in the house with the door shut solid behind her, sliding down to sit, her notebook pressing to her *thumpthumpthump*ing heart.

CHAPTER FOUR

Thumpthumpthump.

Thump-thump-thump.

Thump. Thump. Thump.

Mattie peeks out the kitchen window, looks past the garden and up the rise.

There is a girl out there. A tall girl. A teenager-looking girl, standing up by Uncle Potluck's rock, holding a yellow toolbox, staring down the rise to the porch door. Thinking, probably, about the crazy baby person she has just seen disappear behind it.

"What is it, Mattie Mae? Have we got marauders again?" Uncle Potluck is standing at the stove, stirring something tomato-smelling in a tall white pot.

"Marauders?" asks Mattie.

Uncle Potluck taps his spoon on the pot rim. "Marauders," he says. "Villains. Pirates. Plunderers of booty. Profiteers set on thieving our valuables. Are they out there again?"

Mattie turns her eyes back to the window. The teenager-looking girl is walking around the rock, looking at the yard from one angle and then another.

"There's a girl out there," Mattie says.

"Does she have a peg leg?" he asks, and Mattie can't help laughing.

"No, she does not have a peg leg."

He wipes his brow, playing relief. "Probably just Crystal's niece, then," he says.

Crystal Sweet rents the house out back. Always she's asking Uncle Potluck to come check on her thermostat or look at her pipes, but really what she wants is for him to come look at her. Miss Sweet is sweet on Uncle Potluck, Mama says.

"Crystal called while you were outside, asking where my awesome niece Mattie was, because her awesome niece Quincy had come to visit," Uncle Potluck says. "She was of the opinion that you two girls should hang out together."

"Hang out?" *Thump thump thump*.

"She proposed that the two of you hang out, yes. Awesomely," says Uncle Potluck.

Out at the rock, that girl—that Quincy—has set her toolbox down. She is fiddling with the latch. Mattie cannot tell if she is awesome, but she knows that Quincy is not young. She looks like she wears a bra.

Mattie crosses her arms over her notebook and presses it to her chest. "I can't hang out right now," she says. Not with a teenage bra-girl like Quincy Sweet, who is right now staring down the rise again, right now probably thinking about how not-awesome and not-teenage Mattie is.

Uncle Potluck nods. "Okay, Mattie Mae," he says. "You do what you need to do. I, for one, am simply relieved to know the yard is not full of marauders. I will sleep easier knowing our valuables are safe and secure."

Mattie pulls her eyes from Quincy Sweet. *Safe and secure.* Mattie will sleep easier tonight, too.

CHAPTER FIVE

ALWAYS MATTIE HAD BEEN SHY. Always school had made her feel skittish and small. Always it had taken a while to warm up to things, to people.

But most nights she had slept easily.

Until fourth grade. Until Star.

Mattie had talked to her once. Said just one word.

In the coatroom, behind the cinder-block wall in back of Mrs. D'Angelo's classroom, Mattie was sitting on the bench half-hid by winter coats, switching her recess boots for shoes. Star didn't see her, wasn't looking for her. Star was looking in coat pockets and backpacks, slipping change out of them, putting that change in her own pocket. Mattie watched Star come up on her backpack. Watched her pull the zipper around and down, watched her reach deep inside and find no change. Saw her find Mattie's own yellow notebook, *PRIVATE* written on it, big and red.

Mattie turned to stone watching Star turn pages. Hearing her say words out loud. *No. Bad. Out. Run.* Star said some words in sound-out ways. *Ah-fray-id* for afraid. *Cast-lee* instead of castle.

Star was reading Mattie's stories.

She was holding Mattie's notebook open flat in one hand, the other hand pointing down the lines, turning pages, reading Mattie's words.

She knows, Mattie thought, though what Star knew Mattie couldn't say exactly. Something important, was all. Something true.

Mattie held her breath and watched, waited for Star to look up at her there in the coatroom. Waited for Star to see her, to read her stories and really see her, and for everything to be different after that.

She'd give Mattie some of the coins she stole, maybe, or ask Mattie would she share her lunch so she didn't have to steal coins anymore.

"Take. Go," read Star. She stopped, looked sideways at the page. "Og-ree," she sounded out.

"Ogre." That was Mattie's voice.

Star saw Mattie then. Saw her for a second and then looked on through her—fist-crunching Mattie's story page, tearing it from the others, letting it drop to the floor with the winter boots. Melted snow sucked up into it and turned it dark.

"Og-ree," Star said. She tore another page and dropped it, too. And another and another, until the floor was thick with pages and the notebook nothing but a twist of wire and the PRIVATE cover. Star shoved that back into Mattie's backpack.

"Og-ree," Star said, and it became a magic word. *Og-ree. Og-ree. Og-ree.* Star grew bigger and bigger until she touched the ceiling and filled the coatroom, and Mattie knew Star could swallow her whole.

CHAPTER SIX

THAT NIGHT, IT RAINS. There is no moon.

Mattie pulls her pajamas on, which she can do in the dark. She does not need to see her pajamas. She knows they are pale green with skinny stripes on them, and that the top has three little mouse-shaped buttons. Eenie, Meenie, and Miney.

The last button hole stays empty. Moe is long lost.

"Poor Moe," Mattie says.

The bedroom she is in used to be Mama's when she was a girl. The furniture had been changed around since then, but soon as they moved here, Mama put it back the way it used to be, sliding the bed under the window and pushing the bureau to the far wall. Once the bed got in place, Mattie had hopped up on it, sat cross-legged watching Mama put the rest of the room to rights. Best to get out of the way once Mama got going, Mattie knew.

Mattie sits on her knees now. Looks outside at the moonless night.

There is still some light out there. Miss Sweet has the night off from hospital work, and her orange car is spotlighted in the rental house driveway. A blue square shimmers in her living room window. Probably she and Quincy are watching TV. Probably some teenager show Mattie has never seen.

There is a light in Mattie's ceiling, too, shining round through a pinkie-size hole. When Mama first got this room, her big brothers—Sonny, Roy, Tommy, and Potluck—had shared the room above. They had drilled a hole in her ceiling, pushed a string down through it, and tied a can on each string end.

The idea was that the boys could talk into the can on one end and Mama could listen on the other, or Mama could talk and the boys could listen. Never really worked right, Mama said. "Nobody ever stopped talking long enough to know if you could hear anything."

Now it is Mama above and Mattie below. Both of them are quiet.

Mama was not quiet at supper. Said Quincy Sweet is almost twelve—just a year older than Mattie, really—and doesn't know anyone in town—just like Mattie doesn't—and can't stay alone in that house when Crystal goes to work the night shift at the hospital tomorrow—just like Mattie wouldn't want to should Mama have to work nights—and doesn't Mattie want to have a sleepover with Quincy?

Mama's hands had sat still on the table. Mattie checked. No piccolo fingers, no plans being made. Wouldn't be too much of a disappointment if Mattie said no. So she did.

"No, thank you," she said.

Quincy looks older than twelve. She probably knows lots of sleepover things that Mattie doesn't. Knows things you are supposed to talk about and things you aren't. Maybe Quincy is the kind who'd come over and change into her pajamas right in front of you, and then you'd have to do the same.

No.

No sleepovers.

Besides, Mattie has other things to do. She has decided she will not only write her custodial wisdom notes, she will memorize them. Then, should anything happen to her notebook, she will still be ready.

Mattie gets the silver notebook from the bureau

top, flicks on a flashlight she has borrowed from the kitchen drawer. Holds the book close, whispers her words back into the pages.

Do not let mops sit overnight in water.

Rinse twice.

Wring out.

Let dry in the sun.

Sometime during her whispering, Mama's light goes out above. Even Miss Sweet's TV light goes black. She should rest, Mattie tells herself. Rest up for tomorrow. Quiet, she lifts her pillow, slides the notebook snug underneath. Safe.

She pulls the covers up. Imagines the custodial wisdom in her notebook rising up like the heat from Uncle Potluck's rock, rising through the pillow and into her, filling her up with everything she needs to know.

CHAPTER SEVEN

THERE ARE TEACHERS at the school today. Mattie did not think there would be. Not yet, anyway. Thought maybe teachers would show up when school started next week. Thought she and Uncle Potluck would have Mitchell P. Anderson Elementary to themselves.

The teachers stop by Authorized Personnel, asking about Uncle Potluck's summer, laughing when he tells them about the prizewinning fish he caught in a backyard puddle or how in July he had visited a barbeque joint in Franklin County and met the queen of England. "Dainty thing, the queen. Ate spare ribs with her gloves on," he says. "Hound dog true."

Some of the teachers tell stories—though most tell them skinny and pale, finishing quick so Uncle Potluck will have time to tell another.

Some of them talk about janitorial issues. Class-room windows that won't budge and furniture that needs moving. Mattie writes those parts down in her notebook, filling up a whole page with things that need doing.

"And who is this?" the teachers ask. Mattie keeps her face to the notebook page, but she knows they mean her.

Uncle Potluck knows, too. Says, "This is my niece Mattie Mae. She'll be starting in Paula's class next week."

And they say, *Welcome* and *Too bad Paula won't be here until Friday* and *It's nice to meet you,* and Mattie says, *Thank you.*

They favor sneakers, the teachers do, most of them wearing white ones with blue or pink trim. One teacher—a man—wears flip-flops. He has hair on his toes. Mattie is glad she will not be in his class. Seems wrong to know your teacher has hair on his toes.

Every teacher who stops by says how lucky Uncle Potluck is to have a helper, and every time he says they are right. Then a pair of high heels clicks up to the Authorized Personnel doorway.

"I see you're a writer," the high-heeled person says. Mattie's heart thumps *how does she know* and *not anymore* at the same time. "I used to carry a note-book when I was your age. I wrote a great many stories in it."

"Mattie Mae," says Uncle Potluck, "this is Principal Bonnet." Mattie waits for Uncle Potluck to say more, but he does not.

"We are very glad you'll be joining us this year, Mattie," says Principal Bonnet. "I try to have lunch with each of our new students. Maybe you could read me some of your stories then?"

Mattie shakes her head at the shoes. "I don't have stories."

Principal Bonnet doesn't say *Speak up* or *Louder* or *Come again*. She just stands there awhile, like Mattie's words are taking their time getting over to her. She imagines that, Mattie does, a picture so strong she looks up to check, half expecting to see her words floating cloudlike in the air.

Principal Bonnet is shorter than she looks in the principal portrait. In the picture, her eyes are crinkle-edged and one of her hands is resting under her chin, but now both her hands are cupped in front of her and filled with doorknobs.

"Robert, the painters took these off when they

did the offices, but they forgot to put them back on. Could you?"

Robert is Uncle Potluck. Takes Mattie a second to remember.

"Yes," he says. "When would be convenient?" He sounds funny, and Mattie turns to look to him. He is standing, formal, his hat wheeling in his hands.

"Anytime. It's not urgent," Principal Bonnet says. "Though if you'd prefer to work without me getting in your way, you could try Thursday. I'll be in a staff meeting in the morning and the office will be empty."

"Thursday morning." Uncle Potluck does not laugh or say that Thursdays are usually when he trains circus lions. He just says, "Thursday morning."

Principal Bonnet clicks inside Authorized Personnel just far enough to hand Uncle Potluck the doorknobs. He has to put his hat on before he can take them, and he does it quick, landing it sideways. He'd like to adjust it, Mattie thinks, but he can't with his hands full of doorknobs. "I look forward to our lunch, Mattie, stories or not," Principal Bonnet says, and away she clicks down the hall.

It is strange-quiet in Authorized Personnel, like

rather than leaving doorknobs, Principal Bonnet took something with her when she left. Uncle Potluck drops the doorknobs onto his desk. Sits, the DIRECTOR OF CUSTODIAL ARTS chair squeaking under him. "So, so, so," he says, filling up the quiet of the room. "Distracting day, this one. Makes it difficult for a man of janitorial disposition to concentrate on the multitude of tasks at hand. What was it I was about to do?"

Mattie checks her notebook. "Third grade window?" she says.

Uncle Potluck raises an eyebrow. "You've been taking notes?"

Mattie nods.

"May I see?"

Mama had asked to see Mattie's old yellow notebook once but had turned her mind to something else before Mattie could show it to her. She hadn't shown it to Mrs. D'Angelo, either. Star had read it, but Mattie had never shown it to anyone.

Mattie sets her janitorial notebook on the desk, turns it so Uncle Potluck can see the list of things that need doing. And he looks so pleased, she shows him other pages, too, notes about toilets and fire alarms and how many classrooms are in the school. Shows him a page she wrote while he was checking his e-mail, about how the whole school was dark-silent this morning until Uncle Potluck jingled his keys in the doors and flipped on the lights. How he checked all the hallways and warmed them up, singing about *eloquence escaping* and *da-doo-doo-doo*, and, even with his traitorous knee, dancing a few steps in each hallway.

Mattie does not show him the front page, the one where she has written Mattie Breen, and Custodial Apprentice underneath.

Not yet.

Uncle Potluck rubs his chin. "I shall have to watch myself now that I know you are recording our custodial endeavors for posterity."

"What is posterity?" Mattie asks.

Uncle Potluck pulls a dictionary off a shelf marked WISDOM and hands it to her.

Posterity is future generations.

Mattie looks up *custodial*, too. It doesn't say anything about doorknobs or mopping or leaky pipes. It says this:

Care or supervision, rather than efforts to cure.

and

Guarding or maintaining.

Mattie likes the idea of caring for the school. Of guarding it. Making it safe.

Uncle Potluck picks up his toolbox. "You coming, Mattie Mae?"

"Just a second," Mattie says. *Doorknobs,* she writes. *Thursday,* she writes. Safe and square.

CHAPTER EIGHT

ALL DAY MATTIE FOLLOWS Uncle Potluck close, watching, making notes for the posterity people best she can. A few times she has to set her notebook aside—like for helping set up the playhouse in the kindergarten and for sink-cleaning in the girls' restroom. It is hard writing neat with rubber gloves on.

She stays close after work, too. Stays close finding radio stations in the pickup truck and plucking garden beans and hunting softball-size pumpkins in the tangle patch. So close, Uncle Potluck turns and bumps her smack into the stone rabbit, toppling both of them to the dirt.

"Mattie Mae," Uncle Potluck says, pulling her back up to standing. "I believe you have earned yourself a rest."

"I'm not tired," Mattie says. Not too tired, anyway.

Uncle Potluck sets the stone rabbit to rights, tugs his hat down low. "What I am about to do, I must do alone," he says.

Mattie blushes thinking maybe he means the bathroom but turns out Uncle Potluck has a report to fill out for Principal Bonnet. "As I'm sure you are aware, great writing is a solitary pursuit."

Mattie nods. She is aware. And she has writing to do, too. Custodial notes she could not write down earlier. "Okay," she says.

Mattie nabs her notebook from its safe spot under the pillow and carries it out to the rise, to Uncle Potluck's rock. She can see Miss Sweet's house from there—its doors all shut and shades pulled down. The yard is quiet.

Mattie lays herself flat on the rock. Lays the notebook flat, too.

Custodial Wisdom: Day Two
Fifteen times thirty

They had been to the cafeteria today. You had to go through the cafeteria to get to the big garbage bins outside, and Uncle Potluck had two trash cans for emptying.

Mattie had tried helping, tried grabbing a handle and rolling a trash can herself, but Uncle Potluck had said no. Said the cans were too heavy and should Mattie try rolling one she might lose hold and get squished and then none of her school clothes would fit right. Instead Mattie followed, looking ahead for obstacles she might move from Uncle Potluck's path.

"There are things you need to know about the Mitchell P. Anderson cafeteria," Uncle Potluck had said.

He was right. There were things Mattie needed to know.

"Tuesdays are pizza days," he said. "That's a single compost bucket day. The gourmands of Mitchell P. Anderson favor pizza, and it is the rare lunch tray that has even a crust left for disposal. Spaghetti and meatballs—that's the same. One bucket. Tacos, submarine sandwiches. All fine." Uncle Potluck adjusted his grip on a can, then kept rolling. "Third Thursday of the month, though, that's Punxsutawney Filet. 'Turkey Drummettes,' Chef DeSmet calls it, but I have seen him out back on many a Wednesday evening armed with a gopher call and a two-by-four. We need two, maybe three buckets on Filet Day."

"Maybe we could bring a bag lunch that day, too?" Mattie said.

Uncle Potluck winked. "Wise choice. Now, could you get that door for me?"

Mattie scooted around him to open the cafeteria door. It was huge, the cafeteria was, with yellow tables jack-knifed in half and pushed against the walls. Fifteen yellow tables. Maybe thirty seats at each.

is four hundred and fifty, Mattie writes in her notebook.

Four hundred and fifty seats. Seems like that would be enough so everybody has a place, but Mattie knows different. Knows there can be a thousand seats and still you might not find the place you belong.

CHAPTER NINE

Og-ree, Star would say.

It wasn't bullying. Not like the bullying on the videos they showed at every school Mattie ever went to. Not something she could tell a teacher or the principal or even Mama. How could any of them understand? It was just one word.

One magic word.

Og-ree, Star would say.

And Mattie would move. Even if she had been sitting with someone nice, Mattie would pick up her lunch and move to another table. Or leave the swings to sit by the kindergarten sandbox. Move to another spot, a spot that was not the one Star wanted.

One little word.

"I said hello."

Mattie jumps. That Quincy Sweet is standing

there by Uncle Potluck's rock, staring at her. Staring, Mattie is certain, even though she isn't looking at Quincy's face. Even though she is looking only at the toolbox Quincy Sweet bounce-bounce-bounces against her thigh.

"Hello," Mattie says. It comes out croaky, like her voice forgot how words get made.

"I tried to be noisy coming up, so I wouldn't freak you out," Quincy says. Quincy's voice is not croaky. It is flat and bored sounding, like she has said these words a billion times before, even though she hasn't.

Mattie rolls off the rock. Pulls her notebook to her lap. *It's okay*, she thinks to say, but Quincy is talking again before Mattie's words come out. "What are you writing?"

Custodial wisdom, Mattie thinks.

Nothing, she thinks.

I can't say that and *take a look* and *go away* thoughts shuffle like playing cards. Before Mattie can pick one, Quincy is talking again. "Don't you know?"

Mattie shrugs. She knows. Of course she knows. It's just . . .

"Writer's block, right? I heard about that. That's what's good about drawing. You don't get drawer's block." Quincy sets her toolbox on Uncle Potluck's rock. Spreads her brown papers across it, too. "I draw still life. Everything you need to know is right there." A stack of carrots thuds on the rock. "Potluck said I could draw these if you and I peel them later." Mattie kneels tall on the grass. She can see the edge of the papers just beyond the stack of carrots.

"Crystal doesn't have any drawing paper," Quincy says. Mattie isn't looking, but she swears she hears Quincy rolling her eyes. "I mean, of course I brought supplies, but I forgot my sketchbook. What kind of person doesn't even have paper?"

Mattie does not know. She also does not know what kind of person calls her aunt by her first name only.

Quincy flips a latch on the toolbox, lifts the top. Instead of wrenches and hammers, there are pencils and paints and art things inside.

"She cut up these grocery bags for me to draw on." Quincy pushes her fingers around in the box and pulls out something that looks like chalk. "They're okay. I can use white on them, which you can't do with regular paper. Besides, I'll only be here a couple of days. I'm going home after my brother's operation is done. He's not going to die, you know."

"I know," Mattie says. She doesn't know any such thing, really, but something about the way Quincy talks makes Mattie feel like she ought to.

"It's just a regular operation for his hernia."

Mattie feels herself blush. She's not sure what a hernia is, but it seems like if you had one, you wouldn't want people knowing about it. Like warts or a bad report card.

Mattie waits for Quincy to say more, but Quincy doesn't. The carrot stack blocks Mattie's view of Quincy's drawing, but she hears the rough of her chalk on the store bags. Hears Uncle Potluck inside clanging kitchen pots, too. Hears a talk-show lady on Miss Sweet's TV telling people to live their dreams and giving them a free electric ice cream maker to take home.

A truck rumbles by on the dirt road out front.

Birds tease in the trees.

Quincy keeps on silent-drawing.

What is Mattie supposed to do now?

Doesn't seem right to leave. Not with Quincy saying what she just did about her brother. Mattie could pretend she has to go to the bathroom, but she'd have to come back after and then maybe Quincy'd be done drawing carrots and start asking more questions. Better to save the bathroom for when she really needs it.

If she lays her notebook flat on the rock, probably Quincy won't see Mattie's writing over the carrot stack, just like she can't see Quincy's drawing.

Mattie puts her thoughts back on custodial wisdom. *The trash company comes on Tuesdays and Fridays.* She remembers the man with the arm tattoos who Uncle Potluck introduced as Chuck Canteloni, King of Garbage, and how Chuck Canteloni had said if ever he found a Queen of Garbage he would be content.

Was that custodial wisdom? Mattie writes it down, just in case. Sticks to just imagining what sort of crown a Queen of Garbage would wear and what their palace might be like. Pictures a Royal Garbage Wedding, too—pictures it so hard she can almost smell the garbage truck, see a JUST MARRIED sign hanging off the back. Pictures a garbage reception. Dancing. Wedding guests in tattered dresses, one of them dabbing a tissue to her eyes, saying how it just proves there's someone out there for everyone.

"Girls!" Uncle Potluck stands on the porch, banging a pot lid with a spoon. "Time to carry in the carrots, please."

Mattie looks up, surprised, almost, to find she is not at the garbage wedding. Surprised, almost, to find herself at the rock and Quincy Sweet there looking up, too.

The apple tree shadow is long on the grass, and Mama's car is in the drive. When did Mama get home?

Quincy Sweet blinks. She is smiling a straight-across smile.

Mattie thinks Quincy will talk then, but she doesn't. Doesn't ask questions, either. Just closes her toolbox.

Mattie closes her notebook, too. Grabs the carrots by their tops. The quiet keeps on. Feels like it would break something to talk now, Mattie thinks. Wonders if Quincy thinks so, too.

Down they go, down the rise, toward the house together, carrying carrots.

CHAPTER TEN

"WANT TO SAY WHY NOT?" Mama asks.

"My stomach hurts," says Mattie. It is not a lie. Her stomach does hurt. Has hurt ever since Mama said again maybe Quincy could come for a sleepover.

Mattie puts down her fork. Ducks her chin. Feels Mama watching her. It is a new thing, this watching, new since they've been at Uncle Potluck's. Mama watching like she's trying to read Mattie's thoughts. If Mama knew Mattie's scaredy-cat thoughts, she'd be disappointed, probably.

So Mattie thinks instead about janitorial safety. About cleaning solutions and how putting two different kinds together can seem like you'd make one super-cleaning kind, but really it can make poison. How you could be cleaning, thinking you're making everything better, and then—just by breathing—you'd be dead.

Mattie keeps thinking this, hoping Mama will move to some other topic, but her eyes stay on Mattie. It's Uncle Potluck who shifts Mama's look, asking how her new job is going.

"It's good," Mama says, finally. "I felt comfortable right away. It helps to have worked at a hospital before—not like my first job at St. Andrew's. Did I ever tell you about that, Potluck?"

Mattie has not heard about it, either.

"It was when I was pregnant, right after I moved out—just before you came back from the army. Anyway, it was my first real office job, and I was worried I'd make a mistake and mess things up. That whole first day I said about three words, I was so scared."

Mama scared? Mattie can't even picture it. Imagines a room full of doctors and nurses and ringing telephones, but soon as Mama drops into the scene, she's charging through it, answering phones, fixing patients. Doctors and nurses rush around begging Mama for help.

"That night, I watched that old TV show *ER*. Everyone on that show was so strong and smart. The next day I played pretend—like we used to when we were little, Potluck. I pretended I was one of those *ER* characters." Mama laughs at herself, takes a swig of iced tea. Mattie stays quiet, wanting Mama to tell on.

"I stood straight and talked tough and wrinkled my forehead to show I was thinking about things. And what do you know? After about a week of pretending, people were thinking that I was strong and smart."

"You are," Mattie says, but right then Mama pops out of her seat and clatters the dishes over to the sink, and Mattie is not sure she has heard. Mama hops to the telephone when it rings, too, but Uncle Potluck is closer. Answers, saying, "Hello, Crystal" and "We were just finishing" and "Now, we were just talking about that," which Mattie knows is him getting ready to tell Miss Sweet that Quincy can't do a sleepover because of his niece who is pretending to have a stomachache.

The drawing time with Quincy had been fine, but as soon as they got to the kitchen, Quincy had started in peeling ten times as many carrots as Mattie could. Talking, too, telling Uncle Potluck about the Fourth of July. Telling him how her daddy, Duey Sweet of Sweet's Trucking, stayed late at the baseball game and needed a designated driver and how when he got home, her mother, who Quincy called Nicolette instead of Mom or Mama or Ma or something, how Nicolette made Duey sleep outside in his canoe with only a plastic tarp for a blanket.

Didn't sound upset about it, either. Quincy had a way of talking—flat and dull, like stones dropping *plunk, plunk* in a puddle. Matter-of-fact, Mama called it.

Mattie had looked it up soon as Quincy left.

Matter-of-fact. Relating to or adhering to facts. Literal. Straightforward or unemotional.

What would it be like to be that way? To tell a story *plunk, plunk, plunk,* not caring what people think?

Just like Mama pretending to be an *ER* person, Mattie tries on being matter-of-fact. Sits tall in her kitchen chair, puts a *plunk* in her voice. "She can come," Mattie hears herself say.

"What's that?" Uncle Potluck looks at Mattie. He heard, too.

"For a sleepover," says Mama, grinning. "Mattie said Quincy can come for a sleepover tonight."

Uncle Potluck's eyebrows send a *you sure?* to Mattie, but Mama is already saying, "Good girl," and it is too late, too late, too late to say she is not.

CHAPTER ELEVEN

UNCLE POTLUCK GOES OUTSIDE to gather the last of the tomatoes from the garden.

Mattie should help.

She should.

But instead, she sneaks to her room. If she puts on her pajamas now, before Quincy gets here, she can change in private. Won't have to worry if she ought to be wearing a bra already or if her underwear looks too baby or if there's something else she doesn't even know to worry about just yet.

She buttons her pajama top.

Eenie.

Meenie.

Miney.

"Poor Moe."

Outside, she can hear Miss Sweet's laugh cracking like glass, Uncle Tommy's motorcycle roaring up the gravel drive. It is dark enough outside for the trees to turn shadow. For the moon to hang small and cautious above them.

"Hello, Moon," Mattie says. Listens for a reply.

Nothing.

Probably she needs to be outside.

She would be, too, if it wasn't for that Quincy Sweet. Be out at the rock ledge with Uncle Potluck listening for Miss Moon. Instead, Mattie will be inside listening to Quincy plunking out stuff that should be private. Expecting, probably, that Mattie will do the same.

A door bangs shut over at Miss Sweet's.

Mattie tiptoes into the hallway. It is dark enough that she can stay there, just outside the kitchen, and not be seen. Soon, too soon, she hears Quincy Sweet plunking outside and the *goodbye* blast of Miss Sweet's car horn. Uncle Potluck opens the door then, and Mama comes in, Quincy following, Uncle Tommy following behind that—visiting like he sometimes does, straight from work and still in his firefighter uniform, asking if there's anything left from supper.

Mattie stacks one bare foot on top of the other. Crosses her arms around herself. She shouldn't have changed. Pajamas aren't much different from naked if everybody else around is in regular clothes. She should change back, she thinks, but when she moves, Quincy spots her.

"Hello, Mattie," plunks Quincy.

Mama waves her into the kitchen.

Everyone is waiting. Mattie does not need to see their faces to know they are watching. How far does she need to walk into the kitchen for them to stop? One step? Two? Maybe she can go to where Uncle Potluck is sitting. Hide her pajama'd self behind his chair.

Mattie breathes deep.

Nobody is really looking at her, anyway. Isn't that what Mama says? People are too busy thinking about themselves to notice much about a ten-year-old girl?

One step. Two. Quick all the way to Uncle Potluck's chair.

"Hello, Quincy," Mattie says.

Mama was right. People have their own things to worry about. Nobody even notices her pajamas.

"You missed a button," says Quincy.

CHAPTER TWELVE

BEFORE SHE LEFT for her hospital shift, Crystal Sweet thanked Uncle Potluck for watching Quincy, but he is not watching Quincy. He and Mama and Uncle Tommy are playing cards in the kitchen, and Quincy is in the living room watching Mattie. Staring at Mattie, feels like.

She has her own pajamas on now, Quincy does, but they are not regular pajamas. Not baby pajamas with matching tops and bottoms and mouse-shaped buttons. Quincy Sweet is wearing a T-shirt, big, with SWEET'S TRUCKING printed on it, and a pair of bike shorts. She has long teenager-looking legs, which, even though she has her own sleeping bag that she could be sitting on, she has stretched out long on Mattie's sleeping bag. Mattie is folded up at the pillow end, her legs hugged up to her chest. She can feel her pajama buttons pressing against her thigh.

Eenie.

Meenie.

Miney.

Poor Moe.

"Who is Moe?" asks Quincy.

Mattie blinks. "What?"

"You said *Poor Moe*. Who is Moe?"

She said *Poor Moe*? Out loud?

Matter-of-fact, Mattie reminds herself. Unemotional.

"Moe is nobody," she plunks, or tries to. She does not sound "I don't care," like Quincy Sweet. She sounds like a little kid playing robot. Mattie tries again. "Nothing, I mean. A button. The missing button from my pajamas." Mattie pokes her pinkie through Moe's empty hole.

"I saw that," says Quincy.

Mattie waits for Quincy to say something else.

Quincy doesn't say anything else.

Just waits.

And waits.

Mattie is supposed to say something.

"I named each of these buttons," she says. *Stupid. Baby*. "When I was little, that is. A long time ago."

Quincy is still waiting. "Eenie, Meenie, Miney, and Moe," Mattie says. "Except Moe fell off." This does not sound unemotional. "I don't care, though," she says.

"If you don't care, how come you said *Poor Moe?*" says Quincy.

How come? "Habit."

"So you say it all the time?"

Mattie looks to the kitchen, sending silent messages to Uncle Potluck. *Ask us if we want popcorn,* she thinks. *Tell us to come play cards. Say the house is on fire and we need to evacuate.*

Uncle Tommy slams his cards to the table. "You're in deep now," he tells Uncle Potluck.

"I don't say it all the time," Mattie says.

"Habits are things you do all the time," Quincy says. "Like my dad smokes all the time. Even in the bathroom. And my mom makes the sign of the cross every time an ambulance goes by. She doesn't believe in God anymore, but she crosses anyway. It's a habit from when she went to Catholic school."

Mattie nods. She has done it again, that Quincy Sweet. Secrets about bathroom smoking and God, all plunked out matter-of-fact. Mattie tries again to match her voice to Quincy's.

"I used to say it all the time, I mean."

"Why?"

"Because . . ." Mattie thinks about Moe. Where he is and why he's there. But Quincy is staring.

"It's dumb," says Mattie. "It's just a thing I say. Like some people say *Darn!* or *That stinks!* I say *Poor Moe!* You know, um, *Poor Moe! I stubbed my toe!* Or *Poor Moe! I wish I didn't have school today!* Like that."

"Yeah?" Quincy squints at Mattie. Tilts her head.

Mattie swallows. "Yeah."

There's a clock in the living room. It's behind Mattie and she can't see it, but she hears it now, loud as gunshots. *Tock Tock Tock Tock.* Finally Quincy speaks.

"How old *are* you?"

CHAPTER THIRTEEN

UNCLE POTLUCK SAYS they can watch a movie, and when Quincy asks, "What do you want to watch?" and Mattie says, "I don't care," it is the first time that night Mattie's words sound solid and flat, *plunk plunk plunk*, like for true she does not care. But in her head there are other words. Wobbly ones she wishes she could say.

I'm sorry, Moe.

So Mattie waits.

She waits through two bowls of popcorn and one movie and Quincy snoring quiet *swee swee swee* three hundred times. Uncle Tommy driving away on his motorcycle and Uncle Potluck humming "Taps" and Mama saying *Good night*. Waits until she is sure that everyone is sleeping.

Then Mattie sneaks to her room.

Finds her notebook.
Writes the truth.

MOE
by Mattie Breen

Once there lived a button named Moe.
Moe was a mouse-shaped button. He was
stitched to some pajamas with strong
thread.

The pajamas belonged to a girl.
She was not strong. Sometimes at night
she worried. When she worried, she
twisted Moe on his thread until she fell
asleep.

. Moe did not mind.

One night the girl could not fall
asleep. The girl worried and worried. She
twisted Moe for a long time.

The next day, the pajamas went to
the Laundromat.

Moe was in a washing machine. Water flooded in. The other clothes pulled and tugged at him, and Moe's strong thread snapped.

Then everything started spinning, and Moe got washed away into the tubes and wires of the washing machine. It was dark and noisy.

Moe was alone.

He didn't yell for help. He knew he would never be heard.

Moe was lost forever.

CHAPTER FOURTEEN

MATTIE POKES AT A PANCAKE, feels her eyelids window-shading up and down. Yawns.

She got up early, dressing in private before Quincy woke. Now Quincy is up, too, changing in Mattie's room, while Miss Sweet sits here at the kitchen table, telling Mama yes on more coffee, saying soon as Quincy gets dressed they'll be out of Mama's hair, asking *Where is Potluck and what is his deal, anyway?*

"He never talks to me," says Miss Sweet.

"Potluck?" says Mama. "You've got to be kidding."

Miss Sweet swats the air with her hand. Her fingernails are long and purple. "Well, he talks. I mean, whatever. He just doesn't *say* anything. Do you know what he told me yesterday?" Crystal Sweet asks Mama.

Mattie perks up. Maybe Uncle Potluck said something about Mattie helping him at the school.

"He said he met a psychic in the army who taught him how to tell a person's future by the way she eats corn on the cob."

It is not about Mattie. But she cannot help but be interested, wondering what her corncob would say if somebody fortune-told it.

"What did you say to him?" Mama asks Miss Sweet.

"I told him I didn't like corn."

Mama laughs. "I'm sorry, Crystal."

"Potluck laughed, too," says Miss Sweet. She puts on a pouty face.

"More sugar?" Mama asks, and Miss Sweet puts her regular face back on, spoons sugar from the jar.

"You'd think that girl was getting ready for prom, it is taking her so long," Miss Sweet says, not seeing Quincy walk up behind her. Quincy's hair is braided in two and hangs long over her shoulders. She looks younger, Mattie thinks. Like a teenager in a school play pretending to be a kid.

"What's prom?" Quincy asks.

"What's *prom?*" Miss Sweet barks a laugh. "What's prom? Only one of the biggest days of your life!" Miss Sweet puts her hands on Quincy's shoulders to guide her out the door.

"I have pictures," she says.

"I'll show you," she says.

"This will be awesome," she says.

Quincy does not say it will be awesome. "Poor Moe" is what Quincy says.

Poor Moe? Takes Mattie's sleepy head till after the door shuts to figure it out. *Darn*, Quincy means. *That stinks*.

Mama empties Miss Sweet's cup into the sink. "Poor Moe?" she asks.

Mattie does not want to say *That stinks* to Mama. Does not want to tell her what happened to Moe, either, since she never has before. She would have had to explain about Star. Explain how just thinking that word *og-ree* could keep Mattie up all night twisting Moe on his thread. Mama'd be disappointed to have a daughter who worried so much. Who wasn't as strong as she was. Who couldn't get tough when the going did.

So Mattie had waited, hoping she'd never have to tell her. Like she is waiting now.

Sure enough, Mama hops to her own answer. "You two want to have a secret code, that's fine with me. My friends and I used to have one, too. We had to with all these boys around." Mama sweeps her eyes from one side of the room to the other. Mattie knows Mama is seeing it like it used to be, her brothers, Sonny, Roy, Tommy, and Potluck, filling every chair and corner.

"My friends and I used to camp out in the backyard for our sleepovers. Once the boys drilled that hole in my ceiling, they could spy on us, so the tent was the only safe place to go," Mama says. "You'd like that, too, wouldn't you? A bunch of friends, all crammed in a tent together, staying up all night, sharing secrets."

Mattie tries thinking of a whole tent of friends. Sees a tent zipped near to bursting with girls. Is so busy seeing this, almost misses seeing Mama's piccolo fingers until Mama has dashed down the cellar stairs. Mattie can hear boxes sliding on the cement floor, cupboards creaking open. A clunking sound. "Mattie! Come help!"

Mattie comes to help, and Mama hands her one

end of a sack. Once she and Mama get it up the stairs and outside to the lawn, Mama unzips it. Inside is a wrinkled-up nylon bundle, plus some poles and rope and plastic stakes. "My old tent," she says.

She snaps the tent up fast, not even stopping to get a proper hammer, banging the tent stakes *smack smack smack* into the grass with the heel of her shoe. Finds Mattie a garden rock for doing the same.

There's a flicker of tags on the tent seam. Each tag has a warning on it, a stick man showing all the things you shouldn't do with tents, like put them up on cliffs or light fires inside them or get them tangled in electrical wires. Mama had said the tent had been her only safe place. Sure was different for a stick man.

"Too bad your first friend at this house won't be going to your school," Mama says.

At first Mattie doesn't know what Mama means. Then she does. Mama means Quincy.

Mama thinks Quincy Sweet is Mattie's friend.

CHAPTER FIFTEEN

IT ISN'T UNTIL MRS. DIAZ-SMITH calls Uncle Potluck's office saying the drinking fountain outside her classroom has sprung a leak that Mattie realizes she has forgotten it. She had been so busy tent-staking and wondering if Mama was right about Quincy being a friend that when Uncle Potluck said it was time to go to work, she forgot to fetch her notebook from its hiding place under her pillow.

She will have to pay extra attention today. Have to remember everything and write it in her notebook when they get home.

"Grab that bucket off the shelf, will you, Mattie Mae?" Uncle Potluck says.

When going to investigate a leak, bring a bucket, Mattie tells herself. She can remember that.

Down the hallway of Mitchell P. Anderson Elementary they go, Uncle Potluck humming and Mattie imagining what sort of leak they might find. Maybe it would be a big one, a floodlike one, with desks bobbing on waves and books soaked to pulp and Mrs. Diaz-Smith islanded up on a swivel chair clutching her telephone, waiting for Uncle Potluck to rescue her.

You'd get to postpone school for a leak like that.

When they get to the fountain, though, Mattie only spots a couple of splashes on the floor tile, and Mrs. Diaz-Smith isn't even in her classroom. She has left a note saying she's at a recess safety meeting.

"You look disappointed, Mattie Mae." Uncle Potluck hoots as he bends his traitorous knee. He wipes away the splashes, lies down under the fountain to look up at the pipes. "Best to fix things when they're small, before they get too big for fixing."

Fix things before they get too big for fixing. She'll write that down, too.

"Want to give this your janitorial scrutiny?"

Mattie lies down next to Uncle Potluck and looks up at the pipes. On the bottom of the big elbow pipe there is a skinny, silver bracelet-looking thing. It has beads of water clinging to it. Mattie guesses this is where the leak is.

"Top-notch janitorial instincts," Uncle Potluck says. "Now, slide out."

He fits a red pipe wrench around a bolt and turns it tight. "First," Uncle Potluck says, "we shut off the water source. Then—hand me the bucket, would you, please?"

Mattie slides the bucket over to Uncle Potluck, who places it under the elbow pipe.

Shut off water. Bucket under pipe.

"Then we drain whatever is left," Uncle Potluck turns a small nut and loosens the silver pipe bracelet. A splash of water lands in the bucket, along with a few black bits that look like dead worms. "There we have it. Washer deterioration," Uncle Potluck declares.

"What kind of deterioration?"

"Washer. Rubber rings that keep the water sealed off from the pipe joints. These pipes are a little larger than most, so I keep a special washer supply—you'll find a bag of them in the toolbox. A new one of these, too." Uncle Potluck hands Mattie the silver pipe bracelet. Probably it belongs in the trash, but Mattie slips it on her wrist. *Washer deterioration.*

The washers come in a bag of ten, but Uncle Potluck only takes one. Gives the rest back to Mattie.

They're pretty stretchy, the washers are, and she slips one onto her wrist, where it bumps and bounces against the pipe bracelet.

It looks pretty. Like one of those friendship bracelets that some girls wear. Mattie puts a second washer on, and then a third and a fourth, until all nine washers are stacked halfway to her elbow.

What would it be like having as many friends as that?

"An elegant look," Uncle Potluck says.

Mattie feels herself red up. What kind of custodial apprentice sits around pretending she has an armload of friends when she is supposed to be learning about fountain leaks?

"I was watching . . . I—"

"You know, Miss Custodial America wore just such a set of accessories during the talent portion of the 2008 competition. She was a plunger juggler."

"A what?"

"Plunger juggler. Could keep five of them in the air at once."

Mattie grins. "You're joking, right?"

"While singing 'Don't Stop Believin',' if I remember correctly."

Now Mattie is laughing. "She did not."

Uncle Potluck raises his hand like he's swearing to something. "Hound dog true," he says. "It was the unplugged version of the song, of course." He tries staying serious, but a grin cracks across his face, too.

"Those washers will need to go back to Authorized Personnel, I'm afraid." Uncle Potluck sets the pipe wrench back in his toolbox. "They are still fit for duty and are the property of Mitchell P. Anderson Elementary."

Mattie rolls the washers down her arm, one after another. They aren't really friendship bracelets, she reminds herself.

She reaches to take off the pipe bracelet, too, but Uncle Potluck stops her. "I believe you have earned that one."

The pipe bracelet has pretty spots at the edges.

Mattie hadn't noticed them before, when she had all the washers on, too.

"It's a fine-looking bangle, Mattie Mae. Could be one is all you need. For now, anyway."

Mattie does not know if it counts as custodial wisdom, but she knows she will write it down when she gets home.

Could be one is all you need.

CHAPTER SIXTEEN

"HOME AGAIN, HOME AGAIN." Uncle Potluck turns the pickup onto the gravel drive, and Mattie cannot help looking. Looking past the tent. Looking to the rock. Looking to see if Quincy Sweet is up there waiting for her.

She is not.

Which is good, Mattie tells herself, turning the bracelet around her wrist.

It is good that Quincy does not come running out of Miss Sweet's house when Uncle Potluck parks. Does not rush up to the truck door saying, *I was waiting for you.* Or, *I was so bored without you.* Or even, *Poor Moe, it was a long day.*

Good because Mattie has custodial wisdom to write down. Good, too, because she has not figured out yet what would be right to say back.

The sun is warm and there is a breeze. She'll take

her notebook to the rock. And then if Quincy Sweet does feel like coming over and saying hello, she'll see Mattie busy writing, like yesterday, and maybe just start drawing and they won't have to talk at all—or not until Mattie is warmed up to it, anyway.

Mattie heads inside to get her notebook, passes Mama's friend tent and the stone rabbit and Uncle Potluck, who has made his way to the garden. Isn't till she's in the house, door shut behind her, that she hears another door open—Crystal Sweet's door.

She doesn't mean to look, but she does. Turns to look out the kitchen window to see if Quincy Sweet is coming over. Does not see Quincy Sweet coming over at all. Sees her blurring away, dashing to the far side of Crystal's car, ducking behind it.

Hears the *thwack thwack* of a car door handle. "Crystal!" she hears Quincy holler. "It's locked!"

A breath later Miss Sweet tiptoes out in sparkly shoes, her hair tornadoed up on her head, ringlets dancing. She has purpled up her eyes with shadow and swapped her cinnamon lipstick for a cotton-candy shade that matches her dress.

"Hey, Potluck," Miss Sweet sings.

"Don't you look frosted?" Uncle Potluck says.

Miss Sweet smooths her candy dress, looks like she can't tell whether being frosted is good or not. "Just having a little fun with my niece," she says, waving her hand at the car. Then she turns to look at Quincy—or where Quincy would be were she not ducking behind the car. "Should we ask Mattie along?" Mattie hears Miss Sweet say.

Miss Sweet's car is long down the driveway, long down the road, before Mattie feels the window screen on her face, smells the tin-can smell of it. She has been leaning into it, listening. She is still listening, even when Quincy and Miss Sweet are gone gone gone.

Could be any reason Quincy does not say yes, she tells herself. Doesn't have to be that she thinks Mattie is babyish or boring. Could be Quincy and Miss Sweet were going on a quick errand. Could be they were going to the store to get something private. Or maybe even they are out getting something for Mattie, though she can't think what that might be.

But when she gets to her bedroom, she knows that none of those things are the reason Quincy Sweet did not say yes.

Mattie's notebook is out on the bed.

Not tucked safe and secret under her pillow, but

open on the bed, open to the words she had written last night, the words about Moe.

Mattie had put it away. She was sure she had put it away, safe under the pillow. In the morning, when she was getting dressed, she had even checked.

But there it is, out and open.

Poor Moe, Quincy had said this morning, right after she had come out of Mattie's room. *Poor Moe*.

Not *Darn it*. Not *That stinks*.

Mattie pulls the stupid silver bracelet from her wrist. Rubs at the rust it has left on her skin.

Quincy Sweet read her notebook.

And she did not say yes.

CHAPTER SEVENTEEN

SHE KNOWS, MATTIE THINKS. Same as she thought with Star. *She knows.*

Knows what, Mattie still cannot say. Not some horrible secret. There is not something *in* the stories. Just that there *are* stories. That they came from someplace inside of her. That they matter.

She knows, Mattie thinks. *And she does not want to be my friend.*

Out in the garden Uncle Potluck is singing about messages in bottles. About sending an SOS.

She should be with him. Out in the garden, helping. Not thinking about stupid things like stories and friends. Mattie swats the notebook closed, slaps it under the pillow, runs out of the room and down the hall and out into the garden.

"That you, Mattie Mae?" Uncle Potluck peers around a cornstalk.

"I came out to help," Mattie says.

"Can't say there is much to do out here right now. We're even down to the last of the corn. Tomorrow we'll have ourselves a big corn feast. Invite Crystal and Quincy. Tommy'll invite himself. That sound okay to you?"

No, Mattie thinks.

Uncle Potluck pushes his hat back on his head. He wants to see her better, Mattie knows, but she turns her face down toward the garden dirt. "You sure there is nothing I can do to help?" she says.

"Well, there are a few stray weeds here and there. It would be a favor to me if you could rid the place of them."

Mattie nods fast. "Which ones are the weeds?"

"Follow me." Uncle Potluck leads her to the edge of the corn patch, points to a slender yellow blade of grass poking out of the soil. Kneels to pluck it out. Hoots.

Mattie kneels like Uncle Potluck does. Hoots, too.

"I admire your attention to detail, Mattie Mae, but unless you have a traitorous knee, that last part is optional." Uncle Potluck sits on the grass. "You go ahead and weed now. I'll supervise."

There isn't much to weed. She'll be done in two minutes. Maybe three. But Mattie does not want to be done. Does not want to think about anything but being a help to Uncle Potluck.

"How did your knee get traitorous?" she asks, hoping there will be a story behind it.

There is.

"Stella," Uncle Potluck says.

Uncle Potluck has had lots of girlfriends, Mattie knows. Made some of them mad, too. But she can't imagine him ever making one of them mad enough to bust his knee up.

"Stella, Stella, Stella," Uncle Potluck says. "Laziest dog in the United States Army."

"Dog?"

"Dog. Stella was one of a small squadron of pound dogs rescued from imminent demise, brought to Fort Kincade to train with me and my fellow MPs as trackers. It was an honor most of those dogs took seriously. All Stella wanted to take was a nap—there's another one infiltrating the carrot patch, see?"

Uncle Potluck points to a short, scrawny weed. It is nearly dead, but Mattie rushes to pluck it, anyway.

"It was suggested by my superiors that Stella's

lack of initiative was a cry for increased training. I don't think I need to tell you that I was not at liberty to disregard the suggestion of my superiors. Instead, I disregarded that evening's weather forecast. Certain that Stella and I would conclude our training long before the predicted storm blew in, I doused a buddy of mine in Old Spice and sent him out to lay a trail in the nearby woods. Half an hour later he returned, telling me he had made a simple loop through the trees, one so obvious even an unmotivated hound like Stella could follow it.

"Now, the forecast storm was one of many we had endured that week, and the woods were muddy. At first Stella seemed to have caught the scent. After an hour of wandering, though, I was convinced she was lost. And, I am embarrassed to say, so was I. Which is when the storm blew in—complete with light show and sound effects."

"Lightning?" Mattie asks.

"And thunder, which I soon discovered was a particular fear of my hound dog colleague. One boom, and she bolted. I raced after her, slipping and sliding in the mud, barely keeping ahold on her leash when—

bang!—the earth gave way and my right leg dropped deep into a gopher hole. My left leg, unaware of the situation, continued after Stella.

"I will spare you a description of the pain I then endured and the vocabularic offenses I thus unleashed, but I will tell you that with all my yelling and cursing, I also unleashed Stella, who tore off into the woods and—"

There is a buzzing sound, and Uncle Potluck pats his shirt pocket, searching for his cell phone.

Mattie finishes his sentence. "And that's how you got your traitorous knee."

Uncle Potluck hoots as he stands. "Custodial Arts," he says into the phone. "It's on my laptop," he says, heading for the house. "Just a minute."

Poor Uncle Potluck, Mattie thinks. Just trying to help a dog and getting his knee busted. Poor Stella, too.

Mattie pulls a weed from the turnip row. Looks around for another. There are no more weeds to pull. Nothing she can do.

If she were Mama, she'd say the going had gotten tough. If she were Mama, she would get going.

But where is she supposed to go? She cannot follow Uncle Potluck. Cannot write in her notebook. Does not want to go back to her room or to the tent or to the rock on the rise. Instead, Mattie stands there, weeds in her hand, not going anywhere.

Not looking, not looking, not looking at the spot where Miss Sweet's car used to be.

CHAPTER EIGHTEEN

LATER MISS SWEET CALLS from a restaurant.

She and Quincy are eating, she tells Uncle Potluck.

They are having an awesome time, she says.

She's going to skip work tonight, so Quincy won't need to sleep over.

"It's okay," Mattie says.

It is okay.

It will be good to sleep in her bed tonight because she is tired, and it is okay that Quincy isn't coming over after all.

That night Mattie puts her fingers tight around Miney.

"It's okay," she tells him.

She is careful not to twist.

She is careful not to twist for hours and hours.

And then it is morning.

CHAPTER NINETEEN

IT IS THURSDAY.

"D-day," Uncle Potluck says. "Doorknob day."

Mattie is pushing the cleaning cart, listening to its wheels *cla-chunk, cla-chunk, cla-chunk* over the tile floor, following Uncle Potluck down the Mitchell P. Anderson Elementary hallway to the administrative office. The cart has a trash bin on it and a vacuum and slots for spray bottles and paper towels and things for dusting. The vacuum sits tall, so Mattie has to peek around it to see Uncle Potluck, and sometimes she can duck behind it so he can't see her—like when she needs to yawn, which she does every dozen *cla-chunk*s or so. She peeks around again, just in time to see Uncle Potluck signal her to stop so he can salute the painting of Principal Bonnet.

This time Mattie salutes, too.

"Mattie Mae," Uncle Potluck says. "I'd like to request that you leave this one detail out of your otherwise impeccable account of our custodial endeavors. Should our fair principal find I have been saluting her visage, she may not take it in the spirit in which it is meant."

Mattie nods.

"And it seems like maybe I ought to be the only one doing the saluting, too. For propriety's sake."

She does not ask what *propriety* is. Does not want Uncle Potluck thinking there is still some custodial wisdom she does not understand.

Not today.

Today, she has decided, is the day. She will not wait until the weekend. Today she will work hard and do everything right, and at the end of the day, she will tell Uncle Potluck about her custodial apprentice plans.

And he will say that is a very good idea. That she should not bother with lunches and recesses and should stick to janitorial pursuits.

And it will all be okay.

Pay attention, Mattie reminds herself.

"I know that you are a person who keeps her own counsel," Uncle Potluck is saying. "But I am glad to know you won't be recording my saluting for posterity—just in case your notebook should fall into the wrong hands."

Mattie does not think about the wrong hands. Thinks instead about Uncle Potluck's hands, watches them fish his key ring from his pocket, flip key after key till he finds the one for the administrative office.

The main door has a knob on it already. It's the inside doors that don't, Mattie sees. The principal's office door and the storage room door and the nurse's room door.

Mattie *cla-chunks* the cart onto the administrative office carpet, parks it carefully by the reception desk, out of the way where nobody can bang into it. She and Uncle Potluck will clean in here after the doorknobs get put in. Vacuum, dust, do the windows.

Right now Uncle Potluck is hooting, kneeling outside the nurse's room door, opening his toolbox, readying for doorknob installation.

There's a couch in the nurse's room. Mattie can see it from her spot behind Uncle Potluck. She is not tired, she reminds herself.

"Shall we begin?" Uncle Potluck asks.

Mattie's notebook opens to the Moe page, but she flips it fast to a clean one. Writes down everything Uncle Potluck does.

Some of the doorknobs have stems out the back and some are flat. Mattie watches, writes down how Uncle Potluck pushes a stem knob through the doorknob hole and then fits a flat knob onto the other side. How he twists in three screws to secure it.

"Then what?" Mattie asks.

"Then there is one last step, Mattie Mae, for which I will need your expertise."

Mattie sets her notebook down. Wipes her palms on her shirt. "Ready," she says.

Uncle Potluck waves her into the nurse's room and shuts the door behind her.

Mattie stands there. Wonders exactly what her expertise is.

"Okay, now," Uncle Potluck says. "Open the door."

Mattie turns the knob. Pulls open the door.

Uncle Potluck smiles. "Accomplished with dexterity and finesse." Mattie does not smile.

Her expertise is opening a door?

Uncle Potluck's phone buzzes. Principal Bonnet needs him in the faculty lounge to answer questions about the floor-polishing schedule. "Yes," he says formal into it. "Of course."

"Mattie Mae, I have been called into service, but I shall return. Why don't you take this opportunity to lie down for a bit? You look fatigued."

"I could go with you," she says. "I could help."

"Rest," he says. "I am certain I can handle things on my own." Uncle Potluck leaves, pulling the nurse's room door half-closed behind him.

Mattie is certain he can handle things on his own, too. Can handle everything on his own. How is she supposed to show him how much he needs an apprentice if he can do everything fine without her help?

Past the half-closed door, Mattie spies the cleaning cart. She could clean, couldn't she? While Uncle Potluck is at his meeting? That would be a help.

Quick, Mattie goes to the vacuum, thumps it down to the carpet, unspools the cord, plugs it into the socket behind the administrative office door. Zoom-zips the vacuum under chairs, behind the reception desk, into Principal Bonnet's office, stretching to reach as far as the cord will let her.

Done.

Mattie looks back at her work.

The carpet looks exactly the same as it did before. She cannot tell that she has vacuumed at all. How will Uncle Potluck know what a help she has been?

Mattie leans back, clunking her tired head on Principal Bonnet's office door.

She could install the doorknobs! He would see that, for sure.

Mattie hauls Uncle Potluck's toolbox into the principal's office. Checks her notebook.

Stem knob through the hole. Flat knob on the back. Screws twisted in 1, 2 . . . Mattie does what the notebook says, sliding the stem knob through the door hole, fitting the flat knob onto the other side. Pushes in a screw, turns it around until it is tight. If she hurries, she'll be finished before Uncle Potluck gets back.

He'll be proud of her. Will say, *Fine work* and *How will I get along without you once the school year commences?* That's when she'll tell him her plan.

She imagines his face filling with relief, sees him bringing her back to Authorized Personnel, showing

her the special chair he'd already had made for her—
MATTIE MAE BREEN, CUSTODIAL APPRENTICE printed
on the back.

The last screw twists into place. Now all she
needs to do is test things.

Mattie turns the knob, right then left. Watches a
silver tongue poke in and out of the side of the door.
Walks around to the outside doorknob to test that,
too. There's a button on it—a lock. She pushes the
button and the knob stops turning. The lock works.

Now for the final test. Her expertise.

Mattie hurries back into the principal's office
and shuts the door. The vacuum cord is wedged tight
underneath, so she has to push extra hard against it,
but finally the door closes. *Click.*

"Mattie Mae Breen, Custodial Apprentice, will
now demonstrate her door-opening expertise," she
says. But when she turns the knob, it will not budge.

The button, she remembers. She had left it
pushed in. On the other side of the door.

She has put the doorknob on backwards.

Mattie Mae Breen has locked herself in the principal's office.

CHAPTER TWENTY

DAYS PASS AND WEEKS PASS and no time at all passes until Mattie hears Uncle Potluck's muffled singing outside the administrative office.

She will have to call to him and tell him she has locked herself in. Tell him how she is the one who needs help. How even her door-opening expertise has failed.

Uncle Potluck sounds louder once the administrative office door opens, and Mattie hears him full-voice singing about a magic someone he is resolving to call.

"Uncle Potluck," she says. It comes out quiet, but even if she were shouting, Uncle Potluck would not have heard her over all that happens next. All that happens all at once—the vacuum cleaner leaping and a twanging sound like an old guitar and a crash, a horrible crash, followed by words Mattie has heard mostly in movies and on the playground. Words unleashed.

Mattie does not need to see him to know what has happened. Uncle Potluck has tripped over the vacuum cord that she left plugged in by the administrative office door.

"Uncle Potluck?" Mattie calls. "Are you all right?"

There is a pause, long and deep enough to drown in.

Mattie hears a hoot. And another. "Mattie Mae," Uncle Potluck says. "I fear my traitorous knee has turned on me, and I am in need of your assistance."

He needs her.

Uncle Potluck really, truly needs her.

And there is nothing she can do to help.

It is Principal Bonnet who finally helps him. Answers his cell phone call and comes to his rescue. Helps him to his feet and out of the administrative office.

Principal Bonnet who comes back for Mattie, too, knocking gently on her own office door before she opens it.

"I'm sorry," Mattie says.

"He'll be okay," Principal Bonnet says.

Mattie nods. Reaches for the vacuum so she can wrap the cord up like she should have done right off. Like she would have if she was a real custodial apprentice.

"I'll get someone to do that," Principal Bonnet says. "Right now we need to get your uncle to a doctor."

A doctor. Uncle Potluck needs to go to a doctor. Mattie had been picturing him in Authorized Personnel wrapping his traitorous knee with electrical tape. But Uncle Potluck can't fix what Mattie has done to him. He needs a doctor.

Mattie picks up her notebook with one hand. Discovers she is still holding a screwdriver tight in the other.

She could have untwisted the screws.

Could have taken out the doorknob and freed herself and wrapped the vacuum cord up right and saved Uncle Potluck from getting hurt.

She could have fixed everything.

CHAPTER TWENTY-ONE

THIS IS WHAT PRINCIPAL BONNET SAYS. She says, "You can't have brave without scared."

They are in the Boone County Hospital waiting room. Uncle Potluck is in the exam room. Mama is upstairs at her job on the seventh floor but will come down just as soon as she can. Principal Bonnet is on her cell phone, calling the district office, telling them about Uncle Potluck and how he's scheduled for knee surgery next week and how she'll need a substitute custodian. "Yes, I know this was scheduled for after the holidays. Things got moved around," she says.

And Mattie is sitting there, just sitting there, holding her notebook to her belly, like that might stop the twisting in it.

It is her fault Principal Bonnet needs a substitute.

Her fault Uncle Potluck got hurt.

Her fault, all of it.

Mattie tries not thinking about it, about the crash and the thud. About the hooting sound Uncle Potluck made hopping to the hospital wheelchair. Tries not thinking how she said *Sorry sorry sorry* and Uncle Potluck said *Not to worry*—but how he said that low-quiet, his eyes scrunched and wet.

There's a judge show on the waiting room TV. The sound is off, but words that tell what the judge is saying slip across the bottom of the screen. Sometimes they are spelled wrong, those words. "What were you thikining?" it might say, but then the right word follows after, making the correction. *Thinking* follows *thikining*. *Consequences* after *confrequences*.

Mattie does not want to think about consequences or confrequences. Like how the consequence of worrying all night about somebody reading your notebook might be that you are tired and stupid and make mistakes. Like the consequence of even talking to some teenager-looking girl might be that all your plans get ruined. Like the consequence of being such a baby is that someone you care about—

Mattie looks around the room for something else to think about. Lands her eyes on Principal Bonnet's key chain. There's a picture frame on it with a photo of a lady and a goat inside.

"That's me on Mathews Peak," Principal Bonnet says. She is done with her phone call. "My first serious climb. Four thousand feet up."

Four thousand feet up. Mattie tries imagining herself standing on a cliff four thousand feet up. Tries seeing herself smiling mountaintop-proud like Principal Bonnet in the picture, but she can't.

"You were brave," Mattie says. "I'd be scared."

That's when Principal Bonnet says it. "You can't have brave without scared."

"This guy here?" she says, tapping her fingernail on the goat. "He's not scared, so he's not brave. He's just a goat, going about his goat business."

A boy and his mom come through the waiting room. His arm is pressed tight to his chest, like he knows better than to move it.

"Brave," Mattie whispers.

Principal Bonnet shrugs. "Maybe," she says. "What's scary for one person might be easy for another. Could be that boy is the mountain goat of broken arms."

Mattie wants to laugh. It's funny what Principal

Bonnet said. True, too. "If you're scared of hospitals, it is brave to go to one," Mattie whispers to herself, but Principal Bonnet hears. Says, "Otherwise, it's a walk in the park."

"Unless you are afraid of parks," Mattie says.

Principal Bonnet has a tinkly laugh. Like wind chimes. "I guess you're right. If you're scared of parks, it can be brave to walk in one. If you're scared of dogs, it can be brave to pet one. If you're scared of heights, it can be brave to climb." A commercial flashes on the TV, a boy and a girl eating Popsicles, though the screen words say Pompsickles. "If you're afraid of Popsicles, it can be brave to eat one," she says.

"Afraid of Popsicles?" This time Mattie does laugh.

"I'm sure somebody out there in this world is afraid of Popsicles. For her, eating a Popsicle is an act of great courage. For the rest of us? It's just sucking frozen juice." Principal Bonnet holds the key ring up again for Mattie to see. "You know, I didn't just decide that day to go climb a mountain. First I took classes, and then I climbed hills and small peaks and practice runs. Each time, Mattie, I had to do a small brave thing."

The waiting room doors whoosh open, and three plump ladies come in. "She'll be fine, Alice," one of them says. "You'll see."

A small brave thing. Mattie wonders what that would be for a Popsicle person. Looking at a box of Popsicles at the grocery store? Buying it? Opening it up? With mountain climbing there is at least a class to take, a teacher to tell you what to do next.

What if what you were afraid of didn't have a class for it?

What if you weren't even sure exactly what you were afraid of?

How would you know what small brave thing to do first?

CHAPTER TWENTY-TWO

IT IS RASPBERRY, Mattie's Popsicle.

Mama got it at Biggie's Mini Mart on the way home from the hospital. Uncle Potluck had said they should go on with the corn feast, and Mama needed a few things for supper, and had asked Mattie if there was anything she wanted.

For Uncle Potluck to be okay and me to be a custodial apprentice and Quincy Sweet to disappear off the face of the earth, Mattie thought.

"Popsicles," she said.

Mattie's Popsicle is the kind with two sticks, the kind you can break in half and share with somebody else. But Uncle Potluck is hat-down asleep in the back seat now, and Mama says *No, thanks,* so all the way home Mattie sucks on her two-handled Popsicle. Wonders what it would be like to be brave.

"You're dripping," Mama says.

Mattie grabs a tissue from the glove box. "Sorry," she says to the car seat. There is Popsicle juice on her fingers and she wipes that, too, but the raspberry color stays on.

"Is there something you want to talk about?"

There is not.

Mama turns the car up the long gravel drive, and Mattie keeps her eyes on Crystal Sweet's house, watching the windows, watching the curtains, watching all the way up the driveway. Nobody peeks through the window.

"Looks like somebody's been waiting for you," says Mama.

Up on the rise in the shade of the apple tree, Quincy Sweet is sitting at the rock, drawing. Her bag papers are spread out; her toolbox is open. Like the rock is hers. Like she is taking over.

Mattie drops her Popsicle sticks in the grocery bag. Pushes the car door wide.

"Want to bring Quincy a Popsicle?" asks Mama, but Mattie pretends she does not hear.

She will be brave.

She will be brave and she will tell Quincy that rock is hers. She will tell Quincy Sweet to move.

Through the grass and around the garden and past the stone rabbit. *This is my place.* In her head, her voice is strong. *This is my place.* Up the rise and past the friend tent and to the rock ledge where Quincy had taken up every bit of room with her papers and her pastels and her wide-open toolbox. *This is my place.*

"You are in my place," Mattie says. Comes out so loud, it surprises her.

Quincy looks up. Squints.

Mattie squints back. *Move,* she thinks to say. But she doesn't need to say it. Quincy is already stacking her papers, sliding her toolbox over to the far side of the rock.

"That enough room?" Quincy asks. "You going to write some stories?"

"I'm just . . ." Mattie feels whatever brave she had sliding out the bottom of her shoes. "Yeah, I guess. Maybe."

Down at the house Mama is calling. "Quincy? You want a Popsicle?"

Quincy stands. "Sure," she calls back. "You want one?" she asks Mattie. Quincy is plunky-calm as ever. *Like sucking frozen juice.*

"No," says Mattie. "I'm fine."

And Mattie is fine. She tells herself so. She is fine. Maybe not brave and maybe not mountaintoppy, but fine.

And she stays fine until Quincy comes back up the hill, Popsicle in one hand, Mattie's notebook in the other. "Your mom gave me this to bring to you."

Quincy drops the notebook to the rock, where it falls open. A breeze pushes the pages over, one after another. Mattie sees her words. *Wipe clean. Hazard. Couldn't. Alone. Moe.*

There is a crashing sound in Mattie's ears. Crashing like Uncle Potluck crashing, falling. *Alone. Dark. Moe.* Quincy puts her hand down on a page, looks at what's there. Pretends, Mattie thinks, like she has not read it before.

"How come you wrote Moe all sad like that?" Quincy asks.

How come you read my notebook? Mattie wants to

say. But those are not the words that come. "Because it is true."

"It's not true. A button isn't scared in real life. It's plastic. It doesn't have feelings."

Mattie wants to say, *I know*. She wants to say, *I know* and *I have to go now* and *Goodbye*.

But she says none of those things. And she does not leave.

Quincy bites the top off her Popsicle. "I mean, you made it up. You made Moe feel all scared. How come he's not fighting monsters or having adventures or something? You should write that." *Plunk plunk plunk*. "It'd be better."

Quincy keeps talking. Keeps plunking out about how if she were a writer that's what she'd do. She'd write Moe a big brave adventure. Mattie watches Quincy scrape the last lump of Popsicle off its stick. "But I'm not a writer. I'm an artist." *Plunk*.

Draw it, then, thinks Mattie. And the words come out. "Draw it, then."

"I can't," says Quincy. "I only draw real stuff." She sounds less plunky. Disappointed, maybe. "I have to see it to draw it."

"You could try," says Mattie.

"So could you."

I know. I have to go now. Goodbye. Mattie sees the empty Popsicle sticks in Quincy's hand. "Okay," she says.

"Okay?"

Mattie nods. Opens her notebook to the door-knob page. Flips it. "Okay."

Quincy opens her toolbox, pinches out a pencil. She kneels on the grass, stacking her pages on her lap. She looks all crunched up, like a ball of trash paper.

"You can put your papers up here. There is room for both of us," says Mattie.

"Yeah?"

"Yeah."

Quincy sets her pages on the rock.

Moe having adventures. Fighting monsters.

How do you start a story like that?

CHAPTER TWENTY-THREE

THE ADVENTURES OF MOE
by Mattie Breen

Moe was in the washing machine, but he wasn't scared. He was going to have adventures. He was going to

MOE: HERO OF THE WASHING MACHINE
by Mattie Breen

Moe was the toughest button in all of Laundryville. Laundryville was full of lost nickels and buttons and bobby pins and gum wrappers and grocery lists and barrettes and small rocks and rubber bands and Popsicle sticks and

MOE VERSUS THE LINT
by Mattie Breen

Everyone feared The Lint. It was hairy
and it stuck to things, and all the lost
items of Laundryville had a hard time
sleeping because they were afraid that
The Lint would sneak up on them in the
night and swallow them. Moe the button
mouse was afraid, too, but he was tired
of not sleeping. He decided to fight back.
Moe found a bobby pin. "This will be my
sword," he said. Then he

"Then he what?" asks Quincy.

"I don't know," says Mattie, looking up from
the page. Quincy's bag paper is covered with scribble-
overs and cross-outs. "You didn't draw anything."

"I need a model." Quincy sighs. "I wish I knew
where to find a mouse with a bobby-pin sword. Here."
She hands Mattie a stick. "Stand like a brave mouse."

Mattie stands. She holds the stick. She tries to
imagine herself mouselike. And brave.

"That's not right," says Quincy. She circles

Mattie, tilting her head. Staring at her. Mattie wants to shrink to button size. Wishes maybe she was lost in a washing machine somewhere.

"Try poking the stick out," says Quincy. "Pretend you are fighting off The Lint."

Mattie lifts her arm. *I would not fight off The Lint*, she thinks. *I would drop this heavy stick and run*.

"Lean into it. Bend."

Mattie bends.

"Not like that! Not folded over. Bend your knees! Lunge!"

Mattie tries to lunge.

"Like this!" says Quincy. Sharp, she picks up a stick of her own. Thrusts it at Mattie. "Get out of here, you Lint!" she yells.

"I'm not The Lint," says Mattie. She says it quiet, but firm. "I'm Moe."

"Oh yeah?" says Quincy. She hops closer, her sword just inches from Mattie's chest.

Too close.

Mattie smacks Quincy's sword away with her own. *Thwack!* She feels it vibrate in her hand.

Quincy squints. "Okay. You're Moe and I'm The Lint." She swings her stick back at Mattie's. *Thwack!*

Mattie does not think. She thwacks back. "Take that, you Lint!"

"How about I'm Good Lint?" Quincy squints again. "Like, I ran away from The Lint Monster and joined forces with you, and now we're off to fight him?"

Mattie can still feel the sting in her palm from the last *thwack*. It would be good to have Quincy on her side.

"There he is!" Quincy points beyond Mattie, runs, sword high, to the edge of the trees. Mattie runs, too, swift and brave up to a stout oak covered in moss. Her heart pounds. "Take that!" *Thwack!* A chunk of moss sails through the air.

"And that!" hollers Quincy.

Mattie turns. Moss has sprung up on every rock and tree and limb, reaching out to grab them, reaching out—"Look out, Lint Girl!"

"I see it!" Quincy spins, her sword cutting fiercely through the air. *Thwack!*

The Evil Lint is everywhere. Moe is brave. *Thwack! Thwack!*

"Moe! Over here!" Lint Girl is snagged on a washing machine coil.

"I'll save you!" Moe runs hard and fast, leaping over soap puddles and climbing up water pipes. Lint Girl's cape is caught tight in the old machinery's rusty spiral.

"Pull me out!" she cries. Moe pulls, but the cape will not budge. Moe needs to use both hands—but to do so will mean setting down the sword. What if the Evil Lint Monster finds them? And worse, what if this is a trick? What if Lint Girl hasn't really turned good?

"Please!" cries Lint Girl. There is no time to worry. No time to think. Moe drops the bobby-pin sword and pulls. One by one, the strong threads of Lint Girl's cape snap, until finally she is free.

"Let's get out of here." Moe grabs the sword with one hand and Lint Girl's hand with the other. "RUN!" Over again through coils and wires, under pipes and round tubes they run, hearts pounding, panting, running running running, until they crash safe inside their soap dispenser home.

CHAPTER TWENTY-FOUR

It is Crystal Sweet's car, really, that they smack against.

Mattie sinks to the grass, flops to her back. Quincy flops, too, breathes hard.

"I haven't played like that since I was a kid," says Quincy. Feels like Mattie should say the same thing. Except maybe Quincy would say, *You still are a kid*, so Mattie stays quiet.

For a three whole days or thirty seconds or half a lifetime, there is no sound but Quincy's breathing and Mattie's heart *thump thump thump*ing.

It is quiet.

And then it is quiet some more, and Mattie starts to think maybe it is too quiet. Maybe she is supposed to say something.

What is she supposed to say?

What would Uncle Potluck say?

"Uncle Potluck says when he talks to the moon, the moon talks back."

It is not the right thing to have said. Mattie knows as soon as she hears the words.

Quincy doesn't say anything. She just keeps on breathing, no doubt thinking she is too old for this silly little girl and her stories about buttons and moons that talk. No doubt thinking she was right to stay away yesterday.

"What does the moon say?" Quincy asks. It does not sound mean. Or like she thinks Mattie is a baby.

"I don't know," says Mattie.

"Have you tried it?"

"No," says Mattie. "I couldn't—Uncle Potluck said—" She tries remembering that night. "Uncle Potluck said, you have to trust the moon for the moon to trust you." The grass feels cooler now. Cold almost.

"What does that mean?" Quincy asks. "Trust the moon?"

Mattie shrugs. "I think maybe it's like telling a secret," she says. "I think you have to tell the moon something that matters and is secret, and then maybe the moon will tell you something back."

Quincy sits up. Squints down at Mattie.

She's going to tell Mattie she is stupid. Or babyish. Or that Uncle Potluck is pulling her leg.

"Okay," Quincy says.

Okay what?

Miss Sweet hollers then, hollers for Quincy to come inside. She's got something to show her.

"Tonight we'll sleep in the tent," Quincy says. "Tonight we'll tell the moon something and see what happens, okay?" She does not sound plunky. Not a bit.

"Quincy!" Miss Sweet hollers again.

"Okay?" says Quincy.

"Okay," says Mattie. What else can she say?

CHAPTER TWENTY-FIVE

MATTIE STAYS THERE, still, looking up at the sky. What does she have to say to the moon? What can she say with Quincy listening in?

Uncle Potluck would know exactly what to say. If he were up and walking around, Mattie would ask him to join them. Come out to the rise and call Miss Moon and tell her a story so wild and funny and interesting that Quincy Sweet would forget all about Mattie having to say anything.

Except Uncle Potluck is on the couch, resting. Keeping his leg straight. That's what the doctor said would be best. Rest and quiet and waiting until late next week for surgery to fix that traitorous knee.

What would Uncle Potluck say to the moon with Quincy Sweet listening?

Maybe he'd tell about that dog Stella. Or some other army story. Or about how Grandma Breen gave him his nickname. Mattie liked that story. Liked how five-year-old Robert stole his own birthday cake off the table, claiming a bear had come and tried to eat him, but he had convinced the bear to eat the cake instead. Grandma Breen could only laugh. "Boy's as unpredictable as a potluck supper," she said. He was Potluck after that.

Mattie wishes she had a story like that to tell.

Maybe she could tell one of Uncle Potluck's stories. Tell it like it was her own. Not the name story, of course. Or the Stella story. Or the one about taming circus lions with a harmonica. She doesn't know how to play a harmonica, and Quincy might matter-of-fact ask her to. Only story she has, really, is about Moe. And Quincy has already read that. Already sneak-read that, Mattie reminds herself.

She lies there, reminding herself. Doesn't move until she feels something brush against her cheek. The wind has caught up Quincy's drawing pages, has blown one of them to Mattie's shoulder.

The drawing is a mouse button—two holes through his belly—holding what looks like a spatula, though Mattie knows it is supposed to be a bobby pin. It is a better mouse than Mattie could draw, but different than she expected, too. She had expected it to be like a grown-up drawing and it is not.

Other pages are dancing in the windy yard, and Mattie dashes to catch them. One by the cornstalks. Another flapping around the stone rabbit. Another—the carrots—pinned against the side of Mama's friend tent. Mattie gathers the drawings up, brings them to the rock. Stacks the pages, sets her notebook down on top.

Another breeze and the notebook pages flutter, too. New beginnings for Moe flick to cafeteria notes and cleaning tips, then back again past Moe to a fresh page. Back and forth, back and forth, until they all blend together.

"Mattie," Mama calls from her upstairs window. "Mattie? Come put a sweater on. It's getting chilly."

The apple tree shade is slung low, covering Uncle Potluck's rock, stretching itself down to the garden, all the way to the kitchen door.

Inside the kitchen it's warm and steamy and smelling of tomatoes. It's a homey smell, and Mattie breathes it in as she tiptoes past the living room, where Uncle Potluck is sleeping. Holds it in, down the hallway and into her room.

She is so busy holding in that homey smell, she does not notice it at first. A long string, pushed through the ceiling hole, a tomato can tied to its end. Isn't till the string jiggles and the can—*tunk-tunk*—bangs against the bureau top that Mattie sees it.

A tin can telephone, same as Mama's brothers made when she was a girl.

Mattie exhales. Pulls the string taut, puts the can to her ear. It is cool and holds an empty ocean sound, *swoosh swoosh swoosh*, like a seashell. She holds the can to her mouth. "Hello?"

The can joggles in her hand, and Mattie fits it over her ear again, catches a voice midsentence. "—hear okay. Can you, Mattie?"

It is Mama.

"Yes," Mattie says, though she forgets to put the can to her mouth and has to say it again. She shifts the can to her ear. "—isn't working" she hears.

"Wait," Mama says. "When I'm done saying something, I'm going to say *done*, then I'll listen until you say *done*, okay?" Silence. "Done, I mean. Okay? Done."

Mattie puts the can to her mouth. "Okay," she says. "Done."

"Okay." Mama's voice sounds far away—farther than just upstairs—but Mattie can make out her words. "When I was a girl, it was so noisy in this house. Sometimes I felt like nobody was listening. You know?" she says. "Done."

Mattie nods. Says "uh-huh" into the can. "Done."

"I thought it was different for you. I always ask how you are and how your day was." Mattie feels the can pull in her hand. The string tightens. "But then Potluck pointed out that you don't answer. You say you're fine or you change the subject."

The can makes Mama's words fuzzy and hard to figure out. Even through the fuzz, Mattie hears a familiar tone. A tone she has heard when Mama's hands were piccolo-ing. A planning sound, a fixing sound, Mattie always thought. But now it just sounds sad.

"Anyway, Mattie," Mama says. "I have something I have to tell you . . . done."

Done.

Even before Mama says it, Mattie knows it is done. It is all done. Feels her hand shaking, feels the can shaking against her cheek.

"We're moving," Mattie says. She moves the can to catch her words, says them before Mama has the chance. "We're moving," Mattie says again, and it comes to her full force why. "I hurt Uncle Potluck and I ruined everything. I hurt his knee and he can't work and we can't stay, and it is my fault."

Her hand shakes. Her legs shake, bend, lower her to sitting on her bed.

Not her bed. *The* bed.

Not her room. Not her house. Not her yard or rock or garden. None of it is hers. They are moving, and this is not her house.

The soup can tugs in her hand. Tugs. Tugs. Then the string goes slack.

Done.

CHAPTER TWENTY-SIX

"MATTIE," Mama says.

She is at the door of Mattie's bedroom—*the* bedroom—marching in, already talking. "We are not moving. I promised Potluck—"

"When he's better." Mattie says what she knows Mama is about to tell her. "When he's better, after his surgery, then we'll move."

"Not that either. I promised . . . Your uncle made me promise we'd stick around at least until you're in high school. He said it was hard on you, all the moving."

Mama sits on the bed. "Mattie, each time we moved, it was for a reason. I could see things were going to get harder. Jobs that were going to go south or bosses that—it just seemed best to move on, you know? Best for both of us. But Potluck didn't think it was best for you. He thought—he said you were pretending everything was okay for my sake, and that I was pretending I didn't know you were pretending."

"Uncle Potluck said that?"

"Yes," says Mama. "And I *so* did not want to believe he was right. That's why I got you the diary."

Diary? What did her notebook have to do with moving?

"I figured you'd write in it and say you were fine and prove me right. Or not write in it and prove me right. Or write in it and prove Potluck right, I guess— but I wouldn't tell him so. Thing is, you wrote in it, but it didn't prove anything. You just wrote janitor stuff. And that button story. It didn't prove . . ."

Mama goes on talking, but Mattie does not hear. She is stuck hearing *that button story that button story that button story*. Feels like twenty days pass or four seconds or both, Mattie hearing *that button story* before she figures why that matters.

Mama might know about the custodial wisdom from Uncle Potluck, but to know about Moe . . .

"You read my notebook," Mattie says.

"Yes," Mama says. "And I'm sorry. That's why I put up this can phone thing. I wanted to apologize."

"From upstairs?"

116

"I didn't want to see your expression when I told you, I guess. Maybe I was still trying to pretend." Mama looks like she wants to stand up and leave, but instead she stays sitting. Turns her head so she can look Mattie in the eye. "And now I have to apologize for all the moving, too. I'm sorry, Mattie. I'm sorry I was selfish. I'm sorry I made things so hard for you. I'm sorry I made you think we were moving. We are not moving."

Mattie cannot help but ask. "What about when the going gets tough?"

"The tough are going to have to stick around and face things." Mama pats Mattie's hand, then holds it, her fingers still and warm. "Is there anything else you want to ask?"

Mattie shakes her head, then stops.

"When did you read my notebook?"

"When?" Mama seems surprised. "Yesterday morning. After you and Potluck went to work."

"Was it under my pillow?"

"Yes. I searched around for it, and I found it under your pillow."

If Mama read Mattie's notebook, that meant Quincy Sweet didn't.

"I'm sorry," Mama says again.

"It's okay," Mattie says. Quincy Sweet hadn't read her notebook. And Mama had. And now Mama knows. *She knows*, Mattie thinks, but she does not feel a panicky feeling. Mama knows about Mattie's writing. About Moe. About Mattie worrying about things.

And she has said they would be staying.

Together, they would be staying.

"At least I know how to caulk a window now," Mama says. "You were very detailed about it. I actually learned a lot from your writing. Who knew it took three hundred sheets to fill a paper towel dispenser?"

"Uncle Potluck knew," says Mattie.

"Yes," Mama says slowly. "Yes, he did."

Mama picks up the tomato can. "I'll get some scissors and take this thing down. And I'll figure some way to cover up the hole, too, so you can have some privacy."

"Could we leave it up?" Mattie asks. "Maybe we could use it again sometime to talk about something else? Or just to say hello?"

Mama smiles like this is the best plan she has heard in a long time.

"Done," she says.

CHAPTER TWENTY-SEVEN

THEY WOULD BE STAYING. For a long time, too.

Mattie flops back on her pillow. Feels the edge of her notebook underneath. Her custodial wisdom notes would be useless now. Uncle Potluck would not be at the school when Mattie started next week. She would not be spending her lunches and recesses as his apprentice. She does not need the notebook anymore.

What she needs is a friend.

Mattie sits up. If Quincy Sweet had not sneak-read Mattie's notebook, then she had not been faking. Maybe it's even like Mama thinks. Maybe Quincy is a friend. Or the beginnings of one, anyway.

Which means all Mattie has to do is not mess anything up. Not say anything stupid or baby for one more day, and then Quincy will go home to Nicolette and Duey and her hernia brother, and Mattie can say that she has a friend.

It wouldn't be a lie.

She might be alone at Mitchell P. Anderson Elementary—in the cafeteria or on the playground—but she could say to herself that she has a friend somewhere. Could do that all the way up till Halloween, when Quincy is supposed to visit Crystal. Then Mattie'd have to not mess up all over again—but that she could think about later.

Right now what she has to think about is how to get out of talking to the moon in front of Quincy.

Mattie listens for kitchen sounds. Hears Mama laughing with Uncle Tommy. She can hear Uncle Potluck, too, sounding the same as if he never did have to go to the hospital. Hears Miss Sweet's glass-shatter laugh. "I know!" she says. "I know!"

Probably Quincy is in the kitchen, too, though Mattie doesn't hear any plunking. She should go out there. Should walk right in and say hello and smile a friend smile at Quincy. Except maybe she'd look too stupid or eager.

It is just dark enough outside for Mattie to see her

reflection in the window. She tries smiling at it. Big smiles. Little smiles. Stretched-tight smiles like Quincy wears. Makes her look worried, that last one. Mattie shifts her gaze past the window glass to the sky. The moon sits silent by the treetops, like a schoolyard kid hoping someone will ask her to play.

"I'm sorry," Mattie whispers.

More laughter from the kitchen. "Wait a minute, Potluck, that's not how it goes. Listen . . ." That was Uncle Tommy. He'd tell whatever story Uncle Potluck had just finished. Tell it his way. It would be funny, too, maybe even funnier than Uncle Potluck's. The two of them could go on all night like that.

Which gives Mattie an idea. A very good idea.

All she needs to do is ask Uncle Potluck about his childhood days, or get Uncle Tommy talking about fishing trips or old girlfriends, and just like that the kitchen would fill up with stories, each one tugging at the clock hands until it got so late that Mattie and Quincy would be half-asleep in their chairs. No time left for anything but getting in their sleeping bags and saying *Good night.* She could manage *good night* without messing up.

For a second, Mattie sees her reflection again. The stretched-tight smile is still there, flashing worry back at her. "It will be okay," she tells her window face.

"I'm sorry," she tells the moon again. Listens then, just in case the moon wants to say she understands. But the moon stays mum.

It sits on the edge of the clouds and waits.

CHAPTER TWENTY-EIGHT

OUT IN THE KITCHEN Uncle Potluck is sitting on one chair, his traitorous knee pillowed up on another. Miss Sweet and Uncle Tommy are at the table, too. Mama stands by the stove, a wooden spoon in her hand. Quincy is not there.

"Plant yourself here by me, won't you, Mattie Mae?" Uncle Potluck says, pulling a chair close up by his side. He has to lean to grab it, and the leaning makes him hoot.

"I'm sorry," she says, so quiet only Uncle Potluck can hear.

"You have apologized enough, Mattie Mae," Uncle Potluck says quiet back. "It's okay."

But it is not okay. "It's in my notebook: unplug cords as soon as you are done using them. It's my fault you tripped."

Uncle Potluck nods, thinking. "Will you add

something else to your notebook for me?" he asks. "Add this: if you are going to practice your fox trot while on the job, first examine the area for potential hazards. Mattie Mae, if I had not been so involved in my singing and dancing extravaganza, I would have seen that vacuum cord right off. I believe we share the blame for this one."

Miss Sweet has been listening. Butts in. "You were dancing?"

"A little," Uncle Potluck says. "There are people who inspire dancing in me. It cannot be helped." He leans then. Kisses Mattie on the top of her head, drops his hat over the kiss spot. It feels good. Like having a Band-Aid on a paper cut.

"Look," Miss Sweet says to Mama. She has pulled out her cell phone. On the little screen is a picture of Miss Sweet in her cotton-candy dress. Next to her is a lady in a purple dress. The lady has on even more makeup than Miss Sweet does, and her hair is tornadoed up exactly to match. "Doesn't Quincy look fabulous?"

The lady is Quincy.

"Yesterday I was telling her all about prom and decided we'd get dressed up in my old gowns and go out on the town." Miss Sweet looks through her eye-lashes at Uncle Potluck. "The waiter said we looked like sisters. He's the one who took the picture."

Mattie looks at the picture again. Miss Sweet is grinning. Quincy is not. She looks matter-of-fact. Or maybe bored. Or embarrassed. Makes sense she didn't want Mattie coming along. Or even anyone to see her.

"I did her up again today. You'll see when she comes over. I don't know what's taking her so long."

Uncle Potluck whispers to Mattie, "Would you retrieve our wayward guest? I'm hungry, and your mother refuses to dish out even a spoonful of stew until all are present and accounted for."

Mattie nods and Uncle Potluck's hat tips over her eyes, but she pushes it back up. Goes to get Quincy. Except Quincy doesn't really need getting because just as Mattie reaches the rental house, the door opens and Quincy steps out. Her face is red, Mattie notices, and not made up.

"I've figured out what I'm going to tell the moon," Quincy says. "Have you?"

"Yes," Mattie says. It is not a lie.

In the kitchen, Uncle Potluck is telling another story. "Unleashed," he says as Mattie and Quincy come in. It's the end of the Stella story, the part where Stella takes off and Uncle Potluck is left alone in the rain.

Miss Sweet pouts when she sees Quincy. "You washed off the makeup."

"It felt fake."

Miss Sweet matches her pout with an arm cross. "You get used to it."

"To continue," Uncle Potluck says.

To continue? There is more to the Stella story?

"I must have passed out, because the next thing I know, it is night and there's a terrible crashing sound not twenty yards away. I was certain it was a bear."

"And you with no birthday cake," says Uncle Tommy.

Uncle Potluck throws a hush-up look at Uncle Tommy. Goes on with his story.

"There I was, hurt and defenseless. I reached for a stout branch, though I knew I could not fight off a bear in my pitiful condition. Closer the sound came. Closer . . ."

Mattie feels herself lean forward. Sees Mama do the same.

". . . when out of the woods charged that goofball dog, galloping full speed, jumping right into my lap, and howling like one of Tommy's fire trucks." Mama laughs and Uncle Tommy laughs and even Quincy laughs. "A couple seconds later, two of my fellow MPs struggled through the bushes. Stella had led them straight to me."

"Lazy dog," says Miss Sweet. "She tricked you! She knew how to track all along."

"Maybe she wasn't lazy. Maybe people just didn't understand her," Quincy says.

Mattie thinks about this. About tricks and understanding. Thinks, too, about how maybe even Stella didn't know what she could do. How maybe she didn't know the truth until she had to.

"Hound dog true," Mattie says quietly. Uncle Potluck smiles. Takes his hat from Mattie's head and drops it back on his own.

CHAPTER TWENTY-NINE

MATTIE IS HALFWAY THROUGH EATING her supper when she hears a rumbling sound.

A shiny black car rumbles up the gravel drive, parks next to Crystal Sweet's orange one.

"Who's that?" Miss Sweet asks.

Uncle Potluck sets his corncob down, leans far around Miss Sweet to see out the kitchen window. Soon as he sees, he shoots back to sitting straight. It is Principal Bonnet.

Mama taps Mattie to get the door.

Principal Bonnet has regular shoes on. And regular jeans. She is not dressed like a principal. Or a mountain climber. Just a regular person. "Hello, Mattie. I wanted to check on your uncle. May I come in?"

Mattie lets Principal Bonnet in. It is weird having a principal in your house—even a regular-looking one. Everybody at the table sits taller, Mattie notices. Uncle Potluck. Everyone.

"Hello," Mama says.

"Hello," Principal Bonnet says. Then she turns to Uncle Potluck. "Sir," she says. And she salutes.

Before Mattie has time to ponder the spirit in which the salute is meant, Uncle Potluck laughs a big laugh, one that shakes his shoulders and his belly and even his knee, so he has to put a hand to it to keep it from hurting. "You know about that?" he asks.

"Of course I know, Robert. I am the principal. I see all."

Miss Sweet humphs, unimpressed. "Potluck can see the future in an ear of corn."

Uncle Tommy slaps the table. "Caught!" He laughs. "Let's see you hound dog true your way out of this one."

For a second, Uncle Potluck is silent. Nervous, Mattie thinks. Can't think of anything to say with Principal Bonnet right here in his kitchen.

But then he does say something. Clears his throat and tilts his hat and says, "Tommy, your lack of faith is a sorry disappointment. Sylvie, would you do me the honor of allowing me to examine your cob?"

Mama pushes her plate to Uncle Potluck. Uncle Tommy waves Principal Bonnet to an empty chair. "Sit," he says. "This might take a while."

Uncle Potluck looks around the table, though Mattie notices he skips looking at Principal Bonnet. Just looks at everyone else and then at the cob on the plate.

"Hmmmmm," he says, lifting Mama's corn with a fork. "Before I begin, it is important that everyone present understand that these readings are merely snapshots, rather than complete prognostication. The cob tells us about this moment, offering a keen and discerning reader clues about the future."

"Get on with it," Uncle Tommy says.

Uncle Potluck holds the corn up high, studies it up and down and around. "I see," he says, and "Very interesting" and "Well, now, how about that?" and, finally, "And there you go."

"Where do I go?" Mama asks.

Uncle Potluck raises his knife, points it at the

base of the cob. "See how these large bottom kernels are nibbled clean off? That indicates a person who is taking root. While these here"—he points to the tip of the ear, where the tiny kernels are bit off willy-nilly—"show hope."

Mattie steals a look at Quincy. She looks bored, Mattie thinks. Everyone else is leaning in, listening. Especially Mama.

"Yes, indeed," says Uncle Potluck. "This is a sign of good fortune. The beginning of a new and satisfying adventure for anyone willing to stand firm and face it."

Uncle Potluck sets the cob down on the plate. Everyone claps, including Principal Bonnet. Uncle Potluck's ears red up.

"Thank you, Potluck," Mama says.

Uncle Potluck shrugs. "Thank the corn."

Uncle Tommy pushes his plate across the table. There are three cobs on it, clean picked, not a kernel in sight. "What am I beginning?" he asks.

"Indigestion," says Uncle Potluck. "The corn predicts Alka-Seltzer. Who's next?"

Me, Mattie thinks. *Pick me. Tell me what kind of person I am. Tell me what I am beginning.*

She thinks it tight and loud inside her head, *me me me*, knowing Uncle Potluck will hear it. But he does not.

What he hears, what Mattie hears, what everyone hears, is matter-of-fact Quincy Sweet plunking, "Me."

CHAPTER THIRTY

QUINCY NUDGES HER PLATE toward Uncle Potluck, but before he can touch it, Miss Sweet snaps up Quincy's cob.

"Let me. She's my niece, after all." She holds Quincy's corn up like Uncle Potluck did. Says *mm-hmm* and *aha*, like he did.

"Okay," Miss Sweet says. "Okay, I have it. Okay, so all these rows are totally straight, see? That says Quincy's future is all mapped out perfectly. Quincy's going to be super-popular. And she'll have lots of awesome boyfriends, and next thing you know she'll be Prom Queen, like I was."

It is the best fortune Miss Sweet can think of, Mattie can tell. She's trying to be nice, but Quincy just watches her dinner plate.

It doesn't move, the dinner plate. Neither does Quincy.

Miss Sweet turns to Mama. "You can just tell she's going to have a lovely figure. She's already in a B-cup."

Mattie crosses her arms over her chest. Sees Quincy do the same.

Miss Sweet doesn't see. She's turned her look on Uncle Potluck. "I was totally flat until I was fourteen," she says. "But girls today mature so much faster. I read it in *People*. They call them 'tweens' now, too."

And then Miss Sweet starts in talking about how tweens wear lip gloss and tweens do texting and how all tweens want is to be grown-up and all they think about is boys. Mattie watches Quincy's face, knowing that all she is thinking about is stabbing her aunt with a fork.

"It's all true," Miss Sweet says. "There have been studies."

"Nobody studied me," says Quincy. It doesn't sound one bit plunky, either.

Miss Sweet starts to say something else, but then Quincy grabs the corncob. Chomps three big bites.

There.

There.

There.

"Study that," Quincy says, and before her cob hits the plate, the porch door is slamming shut and Quincy is stomping out through the garden dusk.

"They're prone to drama, too," says Miss Sweet.

For a minute, the room is quiet. Feels like anything could happen.

Mattie waits.

Waits for Miss Sweet to stand up and go after Quincy. Or Mama to. Or Uncle Potluck to pick up somebody else's cob, maybe even Mattie's cob, and go on with the fortunetelling. Mattie could stay here and listen about her future and never have to go out and talk to the moon at all.

Except none of that happens.

What happens is that Mattie Breen does a small brave thing.

She stands up.

Stands up, everyone looking, and goes outside.

Out into the half-dark, past the bean tepees and tomato cages and the stone rabbit standing lonely guard. Up past the tangle of pumpkin vines, past Mama's friend tent.

Up she walks, up the rise to the woods, to the rock ledge by the apple tree. Up to Uncle Potluck's rock, to Mattie's rock, to the place she knows, even in the half-dark, Quincy Sweet will be.

CHAPTER THIRTY-ONE

QUINCY IS ON THE ROCK. Sitting on it, knees up, arms folded over them, toolbox and bag papers at her side.

"Poor Moe," Mattie says.

Maybe it's a dumb thing to say. Maybe she should have let Quincy talk first.

But Quincy talks second. "Poor Moe," she says. Like a secret code.

She puts her papers on the grass, Quincy does. Drops her toolbox on top of them, making room for Mattie to sit on the rock.

Mattie sits. Pulls close her own knees. The clouds move around some and the light changes, tinting the sky as dark as Miss Sweet's lipstick, Mattie thinks.

Quincy must notice, too. "I wear lip gloss at school," she says.

Quiet.

"I do, too. Or did. Once," Mattie says. "I don't

say much at school. I didn't talk at all that morning. By lunch the gloss had turned to glue. I thought my lips would rip off if I tried to open my mouth."

It is a silly thing to say. So silly, Quincy laughs.

Laughs and laughs like she's going to roll right off the rock. The kind of laugh Mattie can't help laughing with.

"It's true!" Mattie says, still laughing around and around, like a screw untwisting.

Quincy unfolds her legs. Divides her hair for braiding, though she has no bands for the ends and one braid frees as soon as she moves to the next.

A breeze comes, a cloud shifts, slivering a half-light over the trees, opening the darkening sky to the moon.

"It must have heard your lip gloss story," Quincy says.

Maybe. Maybe Miss Moon came out for the lip gloss story.

But the lip gloss story is not the one that needs telling. Not the one Mattie needs the moon to hear. There is another story, a twist-tight story coiled up inside her. And there, with Quincy on the rock beside her, Mattie tells it.

• • •

It starts out backwards from the way she has told it
    before, to Moe and Miney and to herself.

She was so big, it starts. So big I thought she'd
swallow me up.

The story goes on that way. Bottom turning
to top.

The magic word. *Og-ree*.

Notebook pages soaked dark.

Stories fist-crunched.

She, Mattie, had said *ogre*.

Ogre.

Ogre.

How the girl said it:

Og-ree, in a sound-out way.

How the word had been in a story in Mattie's
notebook,

    in her yellow notebook.

How the girl had come upon the notebook in
Mattie's backpack,

    after looking in all the other backpacks.

How she had come in small to the coatroom.

How her name was Star.

How she had come in looking for change.

• • •

The words loosen. Unwind.

Mattie feels herself breathe. Slow and deep, in and out.

"Poor Moe," says Quincy. "That was good. I mean, it was bad. A bad thing that happened. But how you told it was good. No wonder you're a writer," she says. "You're good at stories."

I am, Mattie thinks. It is not a question. It is a statement. A truth. A matter of fact. "I am," she says.

She does not know how loud she says it. Does not know if she has whispered or shouted. Does know that she hears an echo, like the kind you hear on mountaintops. Except this echo is not bouncing off mountains or the woods or the tent or the house. It is not an outside echo at all. It is an inside echo, and Mattie hears it.

Big and round and full as the moon.

CHAPTER THIRTY-TWO

IT IS DARKER NOW. The moon is high above.

Quincy looks up and Mattie looks up, both looking up to the brave round moon.

"Now what?" whispers Quincy.

"You can tell your things," Mattie says. "If you want."

"I did. Before you got out here. I told about Duey and Nicolette and Crystal. All that," Quincy plunks.

All that. Same stories Mattie's already heard. Same plunky things she's already said. It won't work, Mattie wants to tell her. Trusting the moon means saying things that are secret. Things that matter.

She starts to tell Quincy so, but the moon is lighting Quincy's face. She is looking up, twisting her hair in a wishful braid.

Which is how Mattie sees, finally. How she knows that the things Quincy has said do matter.

That is Quincy's secret.

Another light, round and white, bobs off the back porch, through the garden, into the yard, lights up a corner of the friend tent. It stops there. Tilts, then shines back up the rise.

"Mattie?"

It is Mama.

"Up here," Mattie says.

Mama has a flashlight—the firefighter kind that Uncle Tommy uses—and the white of it is so hard, Mattie needs to turn her eyes away, to lift them back to the moon.

"I put the sleeping bags and an extra flashlight in the tent," Mama says. "You want to put on your pajamas?"

"Where's Crystal?" asks Quincy. The lights are on in the rental house.

"Her closet door won't close. Tommy said he'd take a look."

"I'll sleep in my clothes," Quincy plunks. "I don't feel like changing."

"Mattie?" Mama asks.

Mattie shakes her head. "I'm okay the way I am tonight."

Mama stands there, the flashlight pointed at the rock. "I'd better get back," she says finally. "Your principal has a substitute janitor coming tomorrow. She needs Potluck to tell her what has to be done before school starts."

Mattie shields her eyes to see past Mama to the kitchen window. Watches the Uncle Potluck shadow fiddle with its hat.

"He's so shy around her," Mama says. "It's cute."

Shy. Mattie has been called shy. Knows it does not feel cute. "My notebook," Mattie says.

"It's still under your pillow." Mama says. "I didn't—"

"Would you give it to Uncle Potluck?" Mattie says. "My custodial wisdom notes. He can give them to Principal Bonnet if he wants."

"Are you sure?"

Mattie is sure.

"You want me to walk you down to the tent?" Mama asks, lifting the flashlight again. "It's pretty dark out here."

Quincy shakes her head.

"We'll find our way," Mattie says.

They do find their way, Mattie leading, Quincy following, down the rise, to the tent, to the sleeping bags.

The flashlight Mama left in the tent makes it bright enough for Quincy to draw. She pushes some bag pages to Mattie. "I can draw and listen for the moon," she says. "Can you listen and write?"

Probably she can, but for now Mattie just listens. Listens to Uncle Tommy's motorcycle growling down the drive. To Miss Sweet leaving for work. Principal Bonnet saying she'll stop by again tomorrow, if that's all right. Uncle Potluck saying how her visit would be an honor.

Listens to the scritch and scratch of pastels on grocery bags, to the slow and stop of it, and later to the *swee swee swee* of Quincy Sweet's quiet snore.

Listens for something else, too. Something she has not listened for in a long time. She listens for a story, one inside her head that she can write down.

A brave Moe story, maybe. Or she could rewrite an old story. She still remembers some from her yellow notebook.

A breeze ripples the tent sides, flickers the warning labels at the seam. Mattie thinks about the stick man. Wonders if he is enjoying the ride.

She puts her pencil to the rough of the bag paper.

In the morning, when she wakes, Mattie is surprised by what she finds on the paper bag page. What she has written. It is only the beginning of a story, but it is a good beginning, she thinks. The kind that makes you want to know what comes next.

In Ms. Morgan's fifth grade class, you do not stand in front of the blackboard to introduce yourself. And it is not just the new kids doing the introducing—it is everyone. "You are all new to me," Ms. Morgan says.

And so they are moving down the rows, one by one, each person standing and saying their name. Each person standing, saying something interesting about themselves.

There are seven desks before Mattie's. Seven people introducing themselves.

The first two Mattie doesn't remember the name of, her heart beating *whoosh-whoosh-whoosh* in her ears, covering up everything. She made her eyes watch their faces, though, and the second one, a boy, had smiled at her.

Next was another boy. "I'm David Braun," he said. He had a dog, a big one, and he had taken it to obedience school all summer, but still the dog wouldn't sit on command. Makes Mattie think of Stella. *Underneath*, she thinks. *Underneath, maybe*, that dog knows.

Which gets her thinking about the underneath of all these kids in her class, the parts they maybe don't share right away, but are as hound dog true as their hair color or their shoe size or any of the things you can see.

Mattie misses the next girl's name thinking that.

Tells herself *Pay attention*, at the same time thinking that maybe most people aren't going to be paying such close attention when she introduces herself, either. Which makes the whooshing quiet some. Not all, but some.

End of the first row. A girl. Nadia Benedict. She has a box full of fossils under her bed.

Beginning of row two. Mattie's row. Mattie feels her face redding, feels her heart *thumpthumpthumping*.

Katie Culp. She has a twin brother, Joe, and went to the Grand Canyon on vacation.

"Next," says Ms. Morgan.

Mattie wants to look at the next person's face as he stands, but her own face is redding so much, all she can do is look at her notebook. It is a new notebook—a regular one—blue with wire spiraling around one edge. Inside she has written some of the stories she remembered from before and some new stories, too, about the stone rabbit and even one about Uncle Potluck's hat. Mattie puts her hands on the notebook, makes herself listen to the person at the desk in front of her.

"I'm Jed Kim," he says. "I have seven chickens." And then he says their names, smooth as eggs.

"Who's next?" Ms. Morgan asks.

Mattie stands. Keeps one hand on her notebook.

"I'm Mattie Breen," she says. Her voice is quiet, but no one says *Speak up*. Everyone can hear.

"I write stories."

ACKNOWLEDGMENTS

This novel, like my first, began as a picture book—a shy girl, a gregarious uncle, and the magical possibility that if we have the courage to speak about what matters most, a real friend might appear, and listen.

As the story grew to novel length, a number of real friends appeared for me. My critique group members—Kelly Fineman, Susan Sandmore, Myra Wolfe, Ellen Miles, Leda Schubert, and Norma Fox Mazer—read this story countless times and led me to what was hound dog true underneath. Kate Messner and her daughter, Ella, read the book aloud and told me when it echoed. Loree Griffin Burns and Marla Frazee kept me going throughout the process—reminding me to take small brave steps.

I had the good fortune of sharing this work at the Vermont College of Fine Arts Post-Grad Conference, the Vermont Studio Center's Vermont Artists and Writers Week, the Pacific Northwest Children's Book Conference, and a Highlights Foundation retreat. I am grateful to all of those organizations that make it possible for writers to find the time and space to connect with their work.

The folks at Houghton Mifflin Harcourt have been a joy to work with. I am especially indebted to my dedicated and insightful editor, Jeannette Larson, whose editorial wisdom could fill more notebooks than would fit under a king-size pillow.

My thanks to my uncle Hector LeBlanc, who provides care

and supervision for a high school in Farmington, Michigan, and served as my source of custodial expertise. Thanks to Aunt Sharon and Uncle Joe, whose "Camp Sharon" gave me kid-free time to write.

My kids, Jack and Claire, are funny, complex, and inspiring people. They were hushed and shooed often during the creation of this book, and I want to tell them here, in print: Mama loves you more than she loves her manuscript.

Finally, to my husband, Julio Thompson, to whom this book is dedicated: thank you, honey, for your encouragement and support, and for always keeping an eye out for marauders.